ANGELS IN THE DARK

DESCENT INTO DARKNESS, BOOK ONE

SHANNON ELLIOT

ANGELS IN THE DARK

Descent Into Darkness, Book One
By Shannon Elliot

Paperback: ISBN 978-0-5782859-7-9
Ebook: ASIN B09YVMTL3J

First edition June 3, 2022

Edited by Katie Wolf
Cover art by The Book Brander
Formatting by Shannon Elliot

www.authorshannonelliot.com

FROM THE AUTHOR

Reader,

Every artist makes an important decision about their work; to create or not to create diverse and inclusive art. And my goal as an author is to create stories that reflect my readers. I fundamentally believe that everyone deserves to see themselves in the media they consume. I believe everyone deserves their happily ever after.

Angels In The Dark was born from the need to see more of myself, my friends, and my community in books. My characters have battle wounds and emotional scars that they embrace. They transform their trauma, pain, and anger into something more. They love recklessly, and the love they find for each other is validated.

This story is a rebellion through and through.

Enjoy my angels!

Shannon

TO THOSE WHO FEEL BROKEN,
YOU ARE STRONG.
TO THOSE WHO FEEL ABANDONED,
YOU ARE WANTED.
TO THOSE WHO CAN'T FIND HOPE,
YOU ARE NOT ALONE.
YOU ARE LOVED.

"LIFE IS FULL OF HORROR; NOBODY
ESCAPES, NOBODY; SAVE YOURSELF.
WHATEVER PULLS ON YOU, WHATEVER
NEEDS FROM YOU, THREATENS YOU.
DON'T BE AFRAID; PEOPLE ARE SO AFRAID;
DON'T BE AFRAID TO LIVE IN THE RAW
WIND, NAKED, ALONE…"

ANGELS IN AMERICA:
MILLENNIUM APPROACHES
TONY KUSHNER

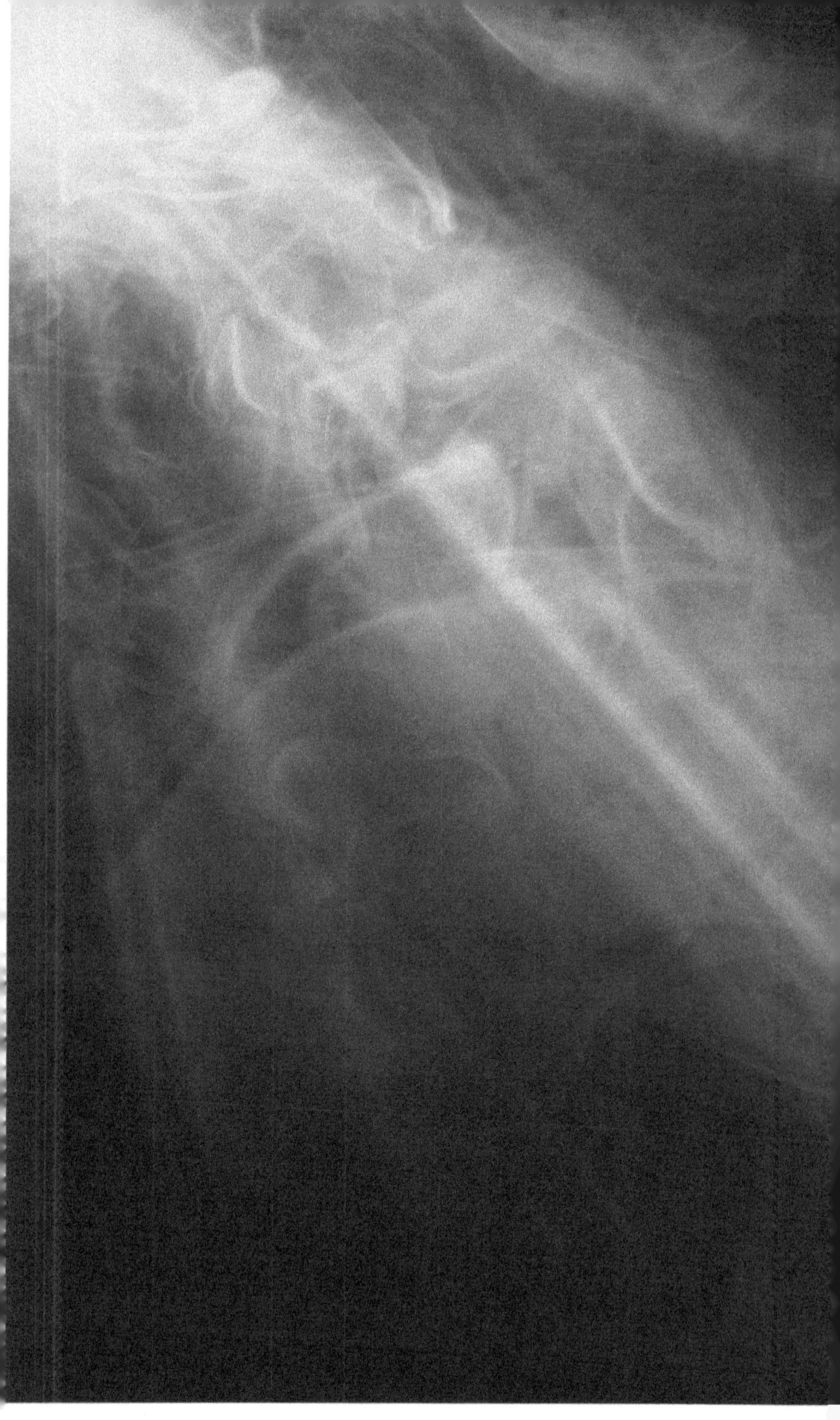

ANGELS IN THE DARK

DESCENT INTO DARKNESS

SHANNON ELLIOT

TRIGGER WARNINGS

Reader,

Not every book is for every reader, and it might be that this book is not for you. Your well-being and mental health come first. So, before diving into this book, I want you to be informed of its contents.

Please note that Angels In The Dark contains the following that may be disruptive to readers: Arson, Being Drugged, Blood, Bodily Harm as Interrogation, Conversion Camp mention, Criminal Underground, Depression, Detailed Torture, Dollification (treating a person like an object for pleasure,) Drug and Human Trafficking, Eating Disorder mention, Edging, Fire, Fatphobia, Gore, Guns, Harassment, Hitmen, Homophobia/Transphobia mention, Hospitalization Mention, Intrusive Thoughts, Kidnapping, Kink, Misogyny, Murder, Needles, Panic Attacks, Pet Play, Pleasure Dom, PTSD, Rage Fueled Outbursts, Rape, Spousal Abuse, Talk of Ruby Play, Threats, Torture, Toxic Masculinity, Trauma, and Violence Against Women.

If you would like further details, have concerns, or feel this list is incomplete, please do not hesitate to reach out to me at authorshannonelliot@gmail.com.

Happy reading!

Shannon

CONTENTS & PLAYLIST

HBIC

Juliana

Beaten down is the only way to fully express the sight before me. The woman is in rough shape. But it's more than the tangled auburn hair framing her face or the sunken features giving her a haunted expression. You can see the story that brought her to my club, Bliss, by merely observing how she carries herself. The weight of her current reality threatens to crush her right then and there.

It's typically this way. The exhaustion. The fear. You can see it in their eyes.

They're never in great shape when they arrive, but it doesn't change the visceral reaction you have when you see someone in this type of pain. Yes, the bruises and neglect aren't pleasant to look at, but it's more than that. It hurts to see how she turns into herself. How the instinct to cradle and protect from unseen threats quashes the trusting nature that must have existed for her once.

That's what's painful. The absence of trust guts me every time.

"Please sit down," I say. Instead of rounding behind my desk to sit, I take up one of the plush chairs in front.

With time, I've made my office a comfortable space. When we first moved in, it was filled with *Playboy* centerfolds and cigarette ads. Now it's my own little retreat inside of Bliss, with lamps bathing the room in a warm light in lieu of the harsh fluorescents or the vibrant neon colors we use out on the floor and stage. The beat-up filing cabinets are covered with an appealing navy peel-and-stick wallpaper, and dozens of framed photos of staff and patrons line the walls.

Good things are supposed to happen here: fresh starts, safety, a new family.

Despite the cosmetic upgrades, it's clear she's hesitant to join me, and her glances back to the doorway threaten to ruin me.

"My friend, Jay, is sitting outside, and I trust him with my life. He won't let anything happen while we're here," I reassure her. "The door is unlocked. You're free to leave at any time. But if you allow it, I want to help in any way I can."

I wait for the shock.

Most people who come here haven't seen genuine kindness in a very long time. It's alarming to realize how little light is needed to change someone. But if I can be that person for them, I want to make an effort.

"I…" the woman mumbles. Her hands fidget, and her gaze bounces between her intertwined fingers and the walls filled with smiling faces.

"You don't have to tell me anything you don't want to." Patience is not my virtue, but I do my best to wait for her to speak. To keep myself from pushing her, I get up to grab a bottle of water from the mini fridge behind my desk. "Why don't we start with your name?"

"Um… I don't…" She takes the water and lowers herself into the chair finally.

"Would you rather use a different name? Sometimes it's helpful. A new name for a new start kind of thing."

It's sad that I know a new identity can give people the relief they need. That being someone, *anyone* other than themselves feels safer than continuing with the memories of their former lives. This woman isn't the first to change her name after arriving at Bliss. She won't be the last either.

She looks relieved. "Sure, yeah."

"How about Roxie? I love the musical *Chicago*, and you seem like a girl with her kind of grit."

"I like *Chicago* too. Roxie Hart is one of my favorite characters, but I feel like I'm more of a Velma Kelly girl." The woman lets out a sound almost like a giggle.

It's the most I've heard her speak so far. It gives me

hope. She'll make it.

"Well, it's your name. Who do you want to be now?"

"Um… Can I be Kelly instead? Maybe Kelly Hart?"

"Sure, honey." I wink and make a note on the pad of paper I grab from my desk.

I add "call Buck" to my to-do list. Fuck Buck. He's a complete asshole and overcharges, but he makes some great forgeries. Plus, he's a halfway decent guy when his head's out of his ass. At least he isn't a misogynistic prick like the last guy. The guilt about breaking the law is a little harder to ignore when you're also having to deal with a guy who calls you "babe" constantly and brags about how good he'll give it to you.

"Now, Kelly. How about you tell me a little about yourself and how you came here to my office, if you're comfortable with that. Then we'll see what we can help you with."

An hour and a half later, Kelly walks out of my office with a job at the club and a place to stay. The extra half hour means I'm running behind, but I feel better knowing she has some support. The house should be good for her since a few other girls on staff are living there. One of our security guys is off to see Buck about the new fakes for her. It's not a lot, but it's more than she had a couple of hours ago.

I inherited Bliss, formerly The Rowdy Cowboy, from my uncle when he died. I was only twenty-two, just out of college, and I was clueless as to why he'd left a strip club to me in the first place. But here we are, six years later, with four locations across Houston.

Somewhere along the way, Bliss turned into a network of safe spaces for women and others with nowhere else to turn. It's for people who can't walk into a mainstream shelter or nonprofit with resources to help for whatever reason. Most of the people who show up at our door are trying to escape something. Many are trying to get away from abusive exes. There are those who have been kicked out of their homes by family when they came out. Others got a bit lost along their path and need someone to help them start over.

Sarah Rose, now simply Rosie, was the first. My best friend Jay and I knew her from college, but we'd drifted apart after she started dating this one guy, Matt. It had been over four years since we saw her last, but when she showed up at the back door of the club sobbing, we knew something was wrong.

It turns out Rosie's ex was a textbook asshole who spent the past four years isolating her from her friends and family. In the years before she came to us, he turned into a belligerent and violent drunk. Then the guy was stupid enough to get caught using drugs at work and was fired, but he never put himself back together enough to move on. He started to take out his anger on her, and she finally reached her breaking point.

When she turned up, it was like no time had passed, and without a second thought, we stepped in to take care of her. We set her up in the spare bedroom of the house Jay and I shared at the time, gave her a job at the club behind the bar, and helped with the police reports and restraining orders. We even beefed up security when the dick decided to show up threatening her.

I guess word spread after that, and people kept coming.

Honestly, it's been great for business. We've never needed to actively recruit new staff. For many of them, we're able to offer something they've never known before—safety and security for sure, but also a community of people who understand.

I've barely finished locking my notes and everything away when Jay walks in.

Standing in the doorway, he looks refined as ever. Jay dresses in a way somehow making him seem larger than his five-foot-six stature. At first glance, you think it's because of the polished shoes and crisp suit he wears as armor. But upon further inspection, it's how his sienna eyes contrast his dark Filipino coloring that captivates you. The multiple piercings in his ears are the only tell that he's not as straightlaced as he tries to appear. With his midnight hair slicked back into a tight bun and faded perfectly on the sides, he looks like a modern-day Bond villain when he smirks.

Right now, it's not a smirk he wears, but the mask he adopts when something is bothering him. To an outsider, he appears almost serene, but there's the tiniest of furrows in his brow. I can tell he's worried by how his lips press a little tighter together.

"Oh, goddess. What now?"

"Sorry. Some guy is becoming a problem on the floor. Rosie texted that he's more than a little drunk and won't keep his hands off the dancers, but he keeps yelling he knows the owner and won't leave until he talks with 'him.'" He scoffs.

I adore moments like this. Anyone truly in the loop knows I'm in charge, with Jay right at my side, but I learned early on that people respect a man's word before they would ever accept mine.

Thus, the invention of "James."

Jay plays the role of James flawlessly. The mysterious playboy club owner typically has at least one dancer hanging off him anytime he's on the floor, namely me, "Bunny." It's a system that works for us. Has since the beginning.

Plus, if all the dancers get pseudonyms, why not us too?

Anytime trouble starts brewing, or someone starts trying to throw their weight around, James and Bunny head over and smooth things out. James acts as a mouthpiece as I whisper sweet nothings in his ear. I'm merely suggesting to him how we should approach the situation. Although now, he's so good at handling things that I'm mostly there for my own amusement.

We've had things get out of control before with patrons who got a little too loud or aggressive, but because of Jay's rough upbringing, he was adamant from the beginning that everyone received at least a little self-defense training. So, no one's ever really been hurt. For the most part, our patrons are respectful and keep their hands to themselves.

The whole charade of James and Bunny is hilarious to everyone on staff since I like to stand in lingerie acting the perfect bimbo girlfriend. The outside world is oblivious to the actual workings of the club. Jay gets a kick out of it since he's got more queer in his pinky finger than the whole of Pride. Passing as the stereotypical cishet man is merely a fun game at this point.

Everyone on staff has a little bit of a dramatic flair. It comes with the job.

"Alright. Give me a minute to get into uniform, and we can go deal with it," I say.

"Sounds good, Julia." He glances at his watch impatiently.

I finish locking everything away and straighten my desk. Before Jay steps out of earshot, I grab his attention.

"Hey. What do you think? Baby doll tonight? Or do we go full-out in the lacy set?"

"For this dude? Baby doll, one hundred percent. He looks like a guy who would get off on that." The grin that lights his face is captivating.

"Perfect. Meet you on the floor."

I make my way down the hall towards the dressing room where all the dancers get ready. I walk into the room and greet everyone cheerfully before strolling to my section. I could have taken on a purely managerial role by this point, but I still love dancing, and knowing the girls is important to me. We spend so much time together that it's hard not to want to know them.

Opening the wardrobe, I search for the dress I have in mind. The baby doll silhouette dress is like magic with how its color shifts in the light—sometimes more blue and sometimes pinker.

One perk of the job is definitely the clothes. I love getting to play dress-up, and it helps that all the lingerie we wear makes me feel sexy as hell.

As I pull the iridescent dress off its hanger, I marvel at the concept—me feeling sexy in lingerie. Years spent in a dance studio scrutinizing every part of my body planted a judgmental voice in my head. Even now, I will occasionally find myself lost in painful memories of underhanded comments from well-meaning adults and crying in dressing rooms at department stores because clothes don't fit. It wears on you.

But when I took over Bliss, when I took up stripping, something changed. I don't avoid looking at myself in mirrors anymore or hide in the bathroom to change instead of out in the open with the rest of the dancers. There's something about having a patron's lustful gaze on me as I dance that makes me feel powerful. My size eighteen body is a weapon of seduction. I can manipulate them because they see something they want but society says they shouldn't desire.

Jay was the first person to ever make me feel like my body was beautiful. We had one night together in college, and the memory of how he described my curves and stretch marks makes me blush every time I remember. It was the first time anyone ever contradicted the negative things I told myself when I looked in a mirror. He saw radiance I didn't think existed, and over time, he taught me to see it too.

Now I look in the mirror and see a body that's lived. Its only purpose is to keep me alive, and it's done a damn good job. Sure, there are still things I am self-conscious of, but for the most part, I'm good. I've found happiness and passion in life because the value of my appearance doesn't hold quite the same grip on my self-worth it used to.

I see a girl with lines beside her dark blue eyes, evidence of laughter and smiles. My curled blonde hair has grown out past my shoulders. Tattoos that wrap across my body from one wrist to the other that each bring back fond memories. My body has kept me alive. That's all I really need it to do.

I finish getting ready with the rest of the girls and inspect myself with the same critical eye from my childhood. But this time, I'm armored in shiny fabric, eight-inch heels, and eyeliner that can kill.

At the doorway to the main floor, I take a deep breath and put my mask in place. The façade that shows no weakness. My true self sits behind it, and it's a comfort to know not everyone gets to see everything. It's a relief knowing I get to keep the most intimate parts of myself close.

I haven't always done this. I've lived most of my life with my heart on my sleeve. I've subjected myself to the needs and desires of others, putting them ahead of my own.

Armor in place, I'm ready to head out to the floor to deal with yet another mess.

Goddess, save us from drunk men.

11

PUT THE GUN DOWN

Jay

There are some people you meet in life who you immediately know are important.

Juliana is my person.

As a kid, I felt like I was "other" compared to everyone else. I didn't quite fit. It wasn't until I found my interest in the arts that things changed. Suddenly, I was being praised for my interest in theater, and my involvement was encouraged by my family. It wasn't until I first confessed my crush on another girl in high school that they changed their minds. And I became "other" again.

My family has a twisted view of how I'm meant to live, and they did their best to beat it into me growing up. One summer I was even forced to attend a fucking camp meant to fix me. Their preferred method of accomplishing this involved a literal swift kick: in the ass, ribs, and head. There's nothing like having full-grown adults with weapons beat the shit out of a little girl to

               SHANNON ELLIOT

teach you a lesson in personal safety.

It showed me the importance of knowing how to protect yourself. The need to defend stuck with me, and it's part of why every employee at Bliss takes a self-defense class when they join. There are too many disgusting men in this world, and I refuse to let a girl get hurt because they don't know how to handle a dangerous situation.

My protective tendencies kicked into high gear the night I met Julia. She was drunk off her ass on vodka, with a guy trapping her on the couch where she sat. Drunk Julia is adorable, but back then she was completely naïve. I pulled her away and carried her back to the dorms. Of course, she demanded a piggyback ride. I slept on her floor that night, and in the morning, I found her to be as adorable when hungover as she was tipsy.

Over breakfast in the dining hall, she announced that we were now best friends.

I've never been able to walk away from her since then.

In nine years of knowing each other, we have been through everything. The death of her parents, my coming out, cutting ties with my bigoted family, and my transition.

Together.

When she inherited Bliss from her uncle, I thought

she was overly-ambitious for wanting to take over running a club, much less a strip club, with no experience. I remember how red her usually sapphire blue eyes were when she came to me overwhelmed and begging for help. At first, I was glad to be a comfort to her. I helped where I could, doing little things like helping restock the bar or auditioning new girls for the club. But the sad little looks and whimpers of frustration broke me down, and I caved only a few months into the endeavor.

Now, I'm all in with her and can't imagine us doing anything else. I love working with her and love seeing my best friend every day.

As much as I adore her, the woman is perpetually late. Time is not a concept she seems to understand. Needless to say, waiting for Julia to finish getting ready so we can deal with the ongoing tantrum happening in the house is not ideal.

I love her too much to complain though. Okay, maybe I complain a little. Juliana is in charge, but I'm her right hand, and I've earned my right to make a well-placed comment here and there with no consequences.

I step out onto the floor, and it doesn't take more than a single breath to realize how out of control the situation is. I breeze by the bar to get a quick update from Rosie while waiting for Julia.

"Give me the quick and dirty?"

Rosie sets down the glass she's cleaning to lean over the bar to give me the update. "I mean, I texted you. You already know most of it."

"Okay, yeah, but run me through it again. I don't want to walk in there unprepared."

Rosie smirks at me suspiciously. Everyone's always thought that Julia and I would end up together, but our relationship isn't like that. I want to keep her happy and safe. I don't need more than that, and I've never wanted to ask. Rosie teases me relentlessly anyway.

"Dude over at table eight is about six beers and a handful of shots in. The lightweight started getting a little rowdy about half an hour ago, but something set him off. I know Gigi turned him down earlier because she had a client scheduled for one of the private rooms. He got real riled up after."

I scan the crowd before settling my eyes on the blond who clearly drank too much. "Did we stop serving him?"

"Of course. We tried, but he started bullying the server, and she got spooked, so she asked for you and Julia to intervene. The guy's been demanding to speak with you too. Well, he's been asking for Jim not James. I'm guessing that's you?"

"Who's working his table?"

"New girl. Stacy, I think?"

"Shit. Well, put in one of the vets just in case. Maybe Richie. Move Stacy over to the bachelorette party on the floor." I figure they'll tip better too, and the girl could use the extra cash. Julia said her daughter has been in and out of the hospital recently. "But check in with Richie at the end of the night to make sure she goes home properly compensated. She's back in school. I don't want her worrying about bills on top of her course load."

"Done. How on earth do you remember stuff like that?" She laughs.

"Julia," I muse. "Anyway, he's new, right? I don't recognize him."

"Yeah, first-timer. Doesn't know the rules."

"Okay. I'll be back. Thanks, Rosie."

It's at that moment Julia walks out, looking stunning as ever. She absolutely glows in the dress she decided on, and a small part of me preens at the fact she took my suggestion.

Since the first time I saw her, she's outshone everyone. She's a presence in every room. She takes up space with her curves and her voice. Her laughter is full-bodied, and when she smiles, it's with her whole face. The woman is absolutely radiant.

And she's walking directly towards me with a playful smile across her lips, her hips swaying in that teasingly seductive way.

Oh, she's planning to have fun tonight.

I make my way to her side, and we head over to the table with the drunken asshole of the night. Even with her looking down at me from high atop her eight-inch heel pedestal, I feel like the most important man in the room. Her arm looped through my own and her hand on my chest settle me before I address the problem maker.

"Hey. I heard you were asking for me?" I drop my voice lower.

I can't help but notice how Julia reacts to the change. I know she likes it when my voice gets all "grumbly," as she describes it. And I won't lie, it's amusing to see her reaction. A shiver rolls through her body, and the way she leans into me would send any man to their knees. She tries to shut it down every time, but I manage to see it. She's so open with her every thought and feeling. Plus, I know her too well at this point.

"Jim!" the guy roars. "Good to see you, man! It's been a while!"

"Name's James, and I'm not sure we've ever made acquaintances before."

"Aw. Come on, man! It's me. Chad. We went to school together. We were in the same frat, remember? I have a very hazy memory of you passed out on the couch and drawing dicks on your face."

I scoff at that one. I have never in my life joined a fraternity. First off, I didn't come out until after college, and second, I only transitioned a few years ago. Hard to join a frat when you don't look like you meet their antiquated membership requirements.

"Yeah, sorry, man. I was never in a frat."

The guy looks genuinely confused at my assertion, but he blazes ahead anyway. "Well, I guess it doesn't matter. Look, I'm looking for my girlfriend, and I think she might have come by here."

I shoot Julia a side glance and brace myself for what we both know is coming.

"Her name's Diana. She's about five-foot-five with auburn hair. I love her to death, but she got this silly idea in her head that she wanted to try something new. I'm worried about her. Honestly, I hope you didn't hire her. She's shit at taking care of shit: the house, plants, anything. She wouldn't be a good stripper either. Better for everyone if I'm able to take her home."

His description reminds me of the girl in Julia's office from earlier. Knowing how Julia will be thinking, handing over that woman to this man is not an option. He's gone too far; he's clearly drunk and rambling. But I can also see the alcohol kicking in and his anger starting to rise up.

"I think you're mistaken. We haven't hired anyone new in a couple of weeks, and no one's been inquiring either."

"Nah, man. I know she was here. I'm able to see it

on my phone. See?" He holds up the device in question with a tracking app pulled up.

Crap. Red flag. I tap Julia to signal to the nearest waitress to grab backup. A stony look takes the place of my formerly amenable expression.

"I think you've had enough to drink. No one named Diana has been here tonight nor anyone matching her description."

"Dude. I know she was here. Tell me where she went." His jaw tightens and his fists ball.

Tensions are beginning to rise, and it's at this point I see the first glint of a gun in the waistband of his pants. I glance up at Julia quickly to see if she's noticed as well, but she seems to be focused elsewhere.

"Sir, do you have a firearm on you?" I let go of Julia and take a step toward the man.

"Of course I fuckin' do. This is Texas."

"Sir, I'm going to have to ask you to leave. We don't allow weapons in our club, no matter what the state says," I growl.

The man stands and steps towards us. He's taller than expected. It's as if his demeanor makes him seem small.

"Tell me where she is, and I'll be on my way. I mean, how would you like it if someone was keeping you from your woman there?" He starts to move in her direction. "She's quite the piece, and I'm sure she'd have no problem leaving your ass in the dust. It'd be easy enough to take her too."

That has everyone's ears perked up. I should have acted sooner. He's too close to her, and there's no way for me to insert myself between the two. Julia holds her ground, but there's a twitch in her eye as she faces off with the man.

"I don't take kindly to threats, sir. Especially towards 'my woman.' I'll repeat myself one more time before there are consequences. You need to leave. Now." I put my hand on his shoulder and try to pull him back.

"Fuck no. I'm not leaving until I have back what's mine."

I miss it. The left hook that comes for me. It lands hard. I'm disoriented, and it takes me a moment to stabilize. When I come back to myself, I see a terrifying sight before me. He has Julia pulled up against his chest with her arm twisted behind her back.

The gun is pointed at her head.

Shit.

"Where. The fuck. Is she."

I really hate when they do this. When their masculinity overrides common sense and they do something stupid.

Like pull a gun.

What is wrong with Julia? She's not usually so careless. It's like she's on a different planet today. Normally someone wouldn't have the chance to grab at her. For that matter, what the hell is wrong with me? How did I let this happen?

I need to focus. If anything happens to Julia…

The rest of the patrons aren't even fazed by what is going on. They're too far away and the music is too loud to hear. Attentions are elsewhere.

Julia looks apprehensive. My heart is pounding in my chest. I can't let anything happen. I don't know what I'd do without her. Unfortunately, this isn't the first time one of us has been threatened, but this is the first time someone has pulled a gun. Knives have slipped in before, but normally we're so careful about checking patrons. The staff here expects us to keep them safe from their pasts. Part of taking in people who need help is protecting them from those trying to hurt them.

Chad presses the muzzle of the gun into Julia's hair, and I see her tense. She's frozen in fear.

"Look, why don't we just… put the gun away," I say, trying to soothe him. "And we can figure out what might be going on."

A slight shake of Julia's head tells me I can't give him what he wants. But if the decision is between Kelly's anonymity and Julia's life?

My decision is already made.

Thankfully, his reactions are sluggish because of the drinks. He relaxes a bit. When the gun leaves its place at her skull and he begins waving the firearm around, I take my chance. I'm closer to them than I was, and it doesn't take much to force his hand holding the gun up towards the ceiling.

My main priority is getting Julia out of his grasp. I pull her by her free arm and drag her behind me. The sound of her falling to the ground hits my ears, but I don't turn my focus away from the man in front of me.

He's several inches taller than me, but my hand goes to his neck. I find the pressure points on either side and squeeze. Slowly his body droops in my hold, his inebriation working to my advantage, and I'm able to pull the gun from his loose grip.

Soon Gus, our head of security, is at my side, pulling the man out of my grasp. It takes a bit to let go. This man has my whole body on edge, and violent rage burns in my chest. It's all directed at him.

He hurt her.

"You're leaving, and you won't be back," I state coldly.

Adrenaline still courses through my body as I relinquish our new buddy Chad off to Gus. I sigh as I begin disarming the gun in my hand.

Finding Julia as I look up, I can't help the ache seizing my chest at her form as she sits up. She rubs at her shoulder as if in pain but immediately pulls her hand away when she sees me looking.

"Shit. I don't ever want to see you at gunpoint." I hold out my hand, and she takes it.

"Oh. Come on. I'm fine. I knew you'd get me out of it." She laughs. But there's a tremor in it. Still, she's grinning, and I can't decide if I want to strangle her or hold her tightly.

"Yeah, but I still don't like you being there at all."

"I know, and I love you for it." Her deep breath is telling, but I'm not going to call her on it. Then she kisses me on the cheek before strolling off to the bar as though nothing happened at all.

III

LASH OUT

Juliana

Like the two shots of tequila I downed immediately after walking away from Jay, the rest of the night goes down smoothly. Everyone dances and drinks. Tips are good, and since frat bro Chad left, patrons seem to be in a good mood.

For Kelly's safety, we ask her to get rid of her old phone. Only she doesn't have one like Chad claimed, which is odd. I don't know anyone our age who isn't attached to their phone. I'm starting to get the sense he isn't her ex. There's something she's not talking about. Nevertheless, I give her a new phone from our stockpile and send her home. Gus goes along with her to make sure she gets there safely. He brings up calling the police and filing a report, but I don't want to bring any more attention to Kelly or that guy. She seems to be in complete agreement too.

I almost regret walking away from Jay like that, but the night's kept me busy and I haven't really had time to think about it.

Things begin wrapping up, and by last call it's around one forty-five. I check in with most of the staff and ensure all of the dancers, bartenders, and security team members are set.

Nightly closing duties are the worst part of the job. Going through and tallying up all of the cash coming in is satisfying. But checking inventory and making sure everything is clean and reset for the next day is brutal. Especially after being on your feet in eight-inch heels all evening. It's monotonous and meticulous, but it's worth it at the end of the day. It's a great outlet for the energy and adrenaline left buzzing under my skin. Plus, I'm a night owl. The late hours don't really bother me.

I sit in my office going over numbers when Jay walks in and slides into the chair I took up only hours ago with Kelly.

"Julia, we need to talk."

I roll my eyes. "Oh, no." I'm laying the sarcasm on thick, but Jay's stern face doesn't change. He isn't fucking around. I sigh. "Okay. What's up?"

"Earlier. The fight. The gun to your head? It can't happen again."

"No shit, Sherlock."

Jay stands, makes his way to the side bar in the room, and pulls out the bottle of absinthe. Crap, this must be bad if he's pulling that out.

"Julia..."

"Jay," I parrot.

"Julia, that scared the crap out of me." It's not that he won't look at me that has me worried—Jay doesn't do feelings face-to-face well—but rather the tremor in his voice. "I can't lose you. We've never had anyone pull a gun. It's one thing to have drunken men spouting off random shit. But this? I can't... I..."

"It's okay though. I'm okay." I'm absolutely pandering, but I need him to let this go. Otherwise, I'm going to break down, and I don't have time for that. "You dealt with it. I'm safe. And honestly, it was pretty damn hot to see you take him down like that."

"Please don't joke around."

"I'm not. I'm being dead serious."

"Me too!" His outburst startles me.

I don't think I've ever seen him so animated with anger before. It's been a long time since Jay worked himself up to this extent about something. Seeing him like this is distressing. And a little hot, if I'm being honest.

"Jay. What's going on? I get it. Today was a lot, but we handled it. You handled it." I try to keep my tone soothing.

"I know, and I'm thankful nothing truly awful happened. But..."

"But what, Jay?"

"But if something happened to you? I don't know what I would have done. You're my best friend. My person. I don't want to live without you. I can't."

"Jay, you're being a little dramatic. Don't you think?"

"No. I'm really not. I'm fucking serious about this." He lets out a harsh breath. "Julia, I won't lose you over something like a guy waltzing in with a gun, okay?"

There is so much pain in his eyes. It's been a long time since I've seen it there. Not since he cut ties with his family.

"Jay, you won't lose me."

Generally, I'm pretty good at knowing how to comfort people in these moments. This is different though. Jay isn't wrong. He's my person too, and it would be hell on earth to live without him. When your person is hurting, you take on that hurt too. It becomes hard to know how to comfort someone when you're feeling the pain alongside them.

"Jay? Look at me." I've come up to face him.

He slowly turns his face towards me, and I'm taken aback to see the tears hovering at the edge of his eyes. In our nine years of friendship, this is the closest to tears I've seen him in a long time.

"You're not going to lose me. Nothing is going to happen."

I pull him in for a hug, but selfishly I need to feel

him against me. To find the sense of comfort and safety his closeness brings me. I didn't even realize how much I need this, need him, until my body is pressed against his own and I'm safely in his arms.

"How about I come over tonight?" I lean back and brush a stray lock of his dark hair behind his ear. My fingers settle at his jaw, and I trace his features absentmindedly. "You go home and get us some food. I'll finish up here and come over. I'll text Rosie and say we won't be in until the club opens tomorrow at five. We can hang out or whatever. Spend the whole day together. Today was a lot. I get it. But it's one day, right? There's always tomorrow."

"Yeah, right. Sounds good." His head falls to my shoulder, and I soak in the scent of his spiced shampoo.

"Okay. Well, go home, and I'll meet you there in a bit."

Rosie pops her head into the office. A curious look crosses her face before she speaks. "Hey, I'm headed out. Do you need anything else before I go?" She's standing by as I let go of Jay, then he crosses to her.

"I'm good. I have a few things to finish before I close up, but I'm sending Jay off with you. Oh, and we're gonna be in late tomorrow. Probably not until closer to when we open. Kay?"

"Ooh, date night. Love it! Well then, have fun with your shit. I'll see you tomorrow, babe! Come on, Jay

Bird! You have a lady caller to get ready for!" Rosie calls as she skips away.

Jay's distraught face haunts my thoughts as I go about my tasks. It really has been a long day, but it feels like something more is going on. I'm just not sure what yet.

Cash deposited into the safe, I go to grab my various bags and car keys to head out.

Things have come so far since I first inherited Bliss. It leaves me with a sense of accomplishment to see the place empty like this but teeming with an energy speaking of uncontainable life and a fair share of lust. As concerned as I am about Jay, these last moments when everyone is gone are my favorite and I savor the quiet.

Darkness follows me as I make my way through the club turning off each light one by one. I step outside and feel an odd chill come over me. I shake off the feeling and turn to lock the door to the club.

A sudden sharp pain in my neck is the only warning I have alerting me to danger before a firm hand goes around my throat. One moment I'm there with keys in my hand, and the next, I am drooping to the ground, slowly losing consciousness. The loss of control is startling, and as my vision begins to darken, my anxious pulse starts to rise.

No. No. No, no, no.

"Now it's your turn, bitch."

Those are the last words I hear before everything goes dark.

IV

911

Jay

It's truly amazing what a near-death experience will do to a person. Even if it isn't my own. More than ever, I feel a need to step up for Julia. I've always wanted to be a safe place for her. To be the person she knows she can come to when she's hurting or needs help. But today Julia had her life threatened, and those feelings are changing. I've been lingering on the edge of violence since then, but she's been acting like it hasn't affected her at all.

Julia knows how to do that, talk you off of a ledge. She's good at wrangling emotions until you see more clearly. It's what she does. She pulls people together and holds them there. Today, a gun was pointed at the woman's head, and still she is taking care of me. She's constantly doing it, giving and seeing to other people's needs before her own. I want to see her take for herself, to witness her selfishness instead.

The ferocity of my anger thrums a brutal beat in

my skull. I want to inflict a level of violence on the guy from tonight that no sane person should consider, but at the moment, I am convinced I will end his life if given the chance. The desire to feel his throat struggling for breath as I squeeze is strong. My sadistic thoughts of the harm I can inflict on him don't concern me as much as they should.

At some point on the drive home, I started to breathe normally again. But it's been an hour and a half since I left Bliss, and I'm starting to worry. It doesn't usually take her this long to finish up, and the drive to my place is forty-five minutes. But after the one-hour mark, we're well past her normal version of on-time.

It's more than that though—she isn't answering texts or calls.

The rational part of my brain tries to tell me this isn't the first time this has happened. Every other time it ends up being because Julia fell asleep at her desk. She was too tired to drive and took a nap on the couch in her office. Nothing is really wrong; her phone died. Her neighbor might have texted her about her dog, Spencer. Maybe she went by her apartment to go get him.

There are so many things that could be going on.

Finally, I give up on staring at my phone and waiting for her to walk through the door. I get up and grab my keys. Only, I have no idea what I am doing. Do I go back to the club? Her apartment? The anxiety in my chest keeps me frozen, paralyzed by the number of possibilities in front of me.

Stuck with indecision, I call Rosie. She was with me when we left. She should have some ideas about what might have happened, and she is good at coming up with a plan. Although not quite as skilled at following through.

"I'm getting really tired of people not answering my phone calls," I grumble when my call goes through to voicemail.

The clock says it's nearly four in the morning.

Okay, I'll cut her some slack, but I dial again.

There are some shuffling sounds, then Rosie's voice comes through the phone. "Jay Bird. What the fuck. It's the ass crack of dawn. I'm supposed to be asleep."

"I know. I'm sorry. But Julia was supposed to come over to my place. It's been well over an hour since I got home, but she's still not here. I'm worried something is wrong." The words rush out of me in one string.

"Jay Bird, you need to breathe and slow down, okay?"

"Okay." I try taking a shaky breath.

"Start at the beginning." The sleep is fading from her words. Her tone acting as a balm to my fried nerves. "I'm sure you've tried texting and calling."

"Yes, of course I have," I snap. "I've been staring at

my phone since I got home."

"Did you try calling the club directly? The line to the bar or to her office?"

I pause guiltily. "No."

"Then we start there, okay? You call the office, I'll call the bar. If she doesn't answer, call me back."

"I can do that."

"It's gonna be okay, Jay Bird. One step at a time. Her phone probably died or something."

"Yeah. Probably." I'm lying to myself, but it does help with the ache in my chest to hear someone else say it aloud.

"Call me back in ten no matter what. Got it?"

"Yes. Got it."

She hangs up the phone, and I dial the direct line to Julia's office.

I hear the first ring and hope starts to rise that she might pick up, but with each ring, my hope morphs into fear and guilt. The intrusive thoughts come back in full force.

Something isn't right here.

Something happened to her.

Something is wrong.

She's in danger.

Eight calls have rung through to voicemail when Rosie's contact pops up on my screen.

"No luck?" I practically hiss the words even though

she doesn't deserve my ire.

"No, and you can shove your attitude back down your throat, mister."

"Sorry. Something's wrong though."

"Okay. Phones weren't the answer. Next plan."

I hear movement in the background and grumbles, which I'm sure are from Rosie's current partner or fling or whatever.

"I'm sorry for waking you."

"No, don't be. This is what we do for friends. If you think something is wrong, then I'm right here with you until we figure it out."

"Yeah, thanks, Rosie." My foot taps incessantly. I hear the phone jostle on her end as she gets dressed.

"Okay, I'll head straight to Bliss since I'm closer. How about you stop by her apartment to see if she stopped there and then meet me at the club."

"Good. Yeah. I can do that."

"Hey, Jay Bird?"

"Yeah?"

"Breathe. It's gonna be okay."

Something in me says it won't be.

I find Julia's dog, Spencer, napping on the bed at the apartment. I give him a quick pet after taking him outside, which is more for my benefit than his, and a treat before leaving for the club.

During the drive over, I can't stop thinking about the events of the night. Every detail is on replay in my mind like a movie on the silver screen. The way she looked in her iridescent dress. Her bright smile that lasted through the night, even after Chad pulled a gun on her.

Pulling into the club's parking lot, I immediately spot Rosie's truck. So at least she made it here. Next, I spot Julia's car.

That's not good.

I'm out of my truck before it even fully settles into park and head straight for the entrance. The door is unlocked, but it's expected since Rosie, and hopefully Julia, is here.

But why wouldn't Rosie have called me?

When I enter the main room, I don't expect to see a rumpled, pacing Rosie with her dark umber hair in a messy bun, dressed in Star Wars pajama bottoms, a tank top, and dalmatian slippers.

"Oh, Jay!" She's startled, and unease takes over. "I think you're right. Come with me."

"Rosie..."

"Follow me, Jay."

"Jay? You never call me Jay."

"Yeah, well, Julia isn't here, and I'm thinking you're

right."

"Shit. Okay. So now what?"

"Well, I was going to check the security cameras, but I don't have a master key to the security room, and I didn't want to go digging around in her office."

"Let's go then."

The fact Rosie is suggesting we check cameras is unsettling. No one really checks cameras unless something awful happens, right? That's stuff cops do to catch criminals.

Walking into the security room is eerie, to say the least. The blue light and flickering screen savers shine enough to light the room ominously. Rosie flicks on the light, but the feeling doesn't dissipate as I hoped it would. That sense of foreboding clings to the air.

I sit down in the chair before the screens and pull up the security camera feeds.

"Okay, we left around what, two fifteen probably?" Rosie says.

"Yeah, something like that."

"Okay, well then let's pull up the footage from around then and see if we catch anything." Rosie's hand comes to her mouth, and she nervously bites at her cuticles.

We sit and scan as the footage speeds by, checking all the internal cameras. Then I see Julia leave her office around two thirty, which does not help the tightness in my chest.

"Okay, well, we know she was here then. When did she leave, and what door did she head out of?"

A little bit more searching, and as usual, she's walking over to the back door, arms laden with the million bags she's used to carrying.

"Switch to the outside cameras at the back?"

"Yeah. The timestamp said… what, two thirty?"

I find the marker in the video for the cameras covering the back door and parking lot, and my breath catches as the footage plays.

"You're seeing this too, right?" I whisper.

"Yeah. The car in the back. It's been there the entire time, right?"

"Yeah."

"Okay, switch to the back door."

I press play, and everything stops.

There she is at the back door, turning to lock up. Our blond Chad approaches, and he stabs something into her neck as he grabs her from behind. Then she slowly starts to sink to the ground, bags dropping alongside her.

We watch as the guy sets her down and walks off. Later, he comes back into view with a silver sedan with no plates. He goes over, gathers her up, then throws her into the trunk. The fucking trunk. Next are her bags, thrown right on top of her motionless body, as if she's no different than the rest of her baggage.

This is too much.

Everything is too much.

The air conditioning grows overwhelmingly loud.

The lights glare brightly.

Images on the computer screens begin to swim.

I struggle to get air into my lungs.

What have I done?

I left her here. This is my fault. I should have stayed and waited with her. I should have never left her alone. I'm supposed to protect her.

I'm supposed to keep her safe.

"Jay Bird, are you okay?" There's a faint voice in the background.

Thoughts crowd my consciousness and consume everything else. I'm no longer in a room with Rosie but in a space of my own; only my racing thoughts and all of the overwhelming sensations surround me. Everything feels too tight, too close, too bright, too much.

"I need you to... look... me... the..." The voice fades in and out. It makes no sense.

The only thing making sense, that feels true, is I deserve this. Whatever this overwhelming guilty feeling is. This is my punishment for abandoning her. Because that's what I've done; I left her, and she's gone. Some Chad took her from me.

"Jay. Look at me." I take in the feeling of warm

hands on my face and turn in the direction of the voice.

"How many buttons are on your shirt, Jay?"

I stare blankly. Only vaguely understanding what the voice wants from me.

"How many, Jay? How many buttons? Can you count them?" I touch where the voice points.

Since when do voices point?

My fingers move across the seam of my shirt and feel for buttons. I start to count.

"Seven?"

"Good. Seven buttons. How many piercings on your ear are there?"

Raising my hand to my ear, I feel the cool metal of the studs and hoops there. I trace over them and count as the voice tells me.

No. Not *the* voice. Sarah Rose. Rosie.

"Four."

"Good. Take a deep breath for me, okay? Can you do that?"

"Yeah."

We sit there for a minute, breathing while I fully process everything.

"Julia is gone."

"Yeah, Jay Bird. She is, but we're gonna find her, okay?"

"Yeah. I will."

"Of course we will. We love her."

"I do."

"I'm gonna call the police, okay? You good?" Rosie's face is full of concern. It makes me feel weak and helpless.

"Yeah. Yeah, I'm good."

I slump in the chair. I prop my elbows on my knees and hang my head in my hands.

She's gone. And I failed her.

V

THE DARK

Juliana

I wake up cold.

At some point, someone took my clothes, leaving me in only my thin undergarments. I've been tossed into a dark room, which feels much like I'd imagine a cell would feel. It's dank and dark. Only a hazy light creates shadows through the room. It's cold. So cold. The sounds around me are the perfect soundtrack for a horror movie. Every creak and groan send chills through my bones.

"Where am I?" I whisper to myself.

I hear shuffling, and then a small voice says, "You're awake. For a while there, we were worried you wouldn't wake up."

"What? Who's there?" I slur. New questions arising with every word uttered.

"Shhh. You need to stay quiet. Otherwise they'll hear." The voice is soothing despite its dry, rough texture.

"Who will hear?"

A loud creak comes from down the hall, and more voices filter in.

"Yeah, that's her at the end. Bring her."

The door to my cell jerks open, and I'm hauled to my feet. Someone tugs at my arm and tightens their hold into a death grip. I realize I'm being prompted to move.

I have no sense of direction, and vertigo threatens to send me careening off an invisible edge. Still, I continue to make my way forward. It takes all of my energy to keep up.

Beyond the cold, the only sensations I feel are the bruising grip my captor has on my arm and the dull throb of scrapes and cuts accumulating on my feet and legs. I know I should be in pain, but my mind is trying to distance me from the feeling. It's trying to protect me in the only way it knows how—by numbing the sensations I should be experiencing. I wonder how long my body will be able to maintain this cover of protection before it all comes crashing back.

Lights in the hallway flicker. It feels like we wander endlessly through a maze of corridors and hallways before reaching our destination. A door swings wide, and bright lights blind me momentarily. As my eyes adjust, I take in the room.

It's a cavernous space that makes no attempt at feeling warm or inviting. A desk and chair sit across from the doorway where we enter, but it's more like a work room than an office. Tools and weaponry hang on the far wall with more crates scattered about. Large pillars support the roof above, and there's a drain at the center of the room surrounded by stained concrete.

Standing behind a desk is a man of impressive stature. In any other circumstance, one might consider him attractive with his dark complexion, but his eyes mask a hidden danger. He's fit. Only his graying hair gives away his age.

This man is a predator. He will kill me. Or at least he'll get close. There's no doubt in my mind. The moment his eyes connect with mine, I know it to be true.

His perusal of my near-naked body is hot. There is a flash of recognition in his eyes, though I know I've never met him before. The way he looks at me is like I'm something to toy with. To him, I am dinner, and this man likes to play with his food. The hunger in his eyes simmers with malicious violence.

There are different types of fear, those of the unknown or imminent danger being the most common. But the fear seizing my body is of another variety. I've never experienced this before. This feeling of being afraid of what it would mean to live through the next moments of your life.

The fear of surviving.

"So, Little John, this is what you bring to the table?" There are razors in his voice, and his tone makes the hair on the back of my neck stand at attention.

Internally I huff.

Little John. How ironically fitting.

Well, I guess at least I know his real name.

"Um... Yes, boss?" The man I know as Chad replies from behind me.

Prowling towards me, the man stops only a foot away. The guard who dragged me here still has a firm grip on my arm, but I feel him flinch when the man stops. It doesn't speak well of a man when even his men are afraid of him.

"Good. Very good."

I don't hear any movement, and the man before me grows visibly aggravated.

"Leave," the man commands, and soon the room is empty. I've collapsed on the ground, unable to keep myself standing, when I feel the toe of his boot push against my chin. My face turns, and I'm forced to meet the gaze of my executioner.

The man looms over me, and I'm able to study him. As I look up, I take in his stocky build. He wants to be intimidating, and he works for it. His face, though, is what chills me to the bone. His gaze is fixated on me.

"You know, I'm surprised. You're prettier than Higley described."

I stay silent. I have a feeling I'll be getting a villain monologue soon.

"You look a lot like my wife when she was younger."

That's shocking to hear. The idea this man would be in a relationship? Doesn't compute.

"Do you know why you're here?"

I remain still, afraid of what his reaction would be to the slightest sound or movement.

"No, I'm guessing you probably don't."

Yup, here's the monologue.

"You see, the club you're working for? The man that runs it? He's been stealing from me." He says all this as if I will know what he's talking about, but I have no idea how this has any connection to Bliss. "I have been having a problem with missing merchandise recently. It seems as though whenever I have something go missing, it ends up at that little club. Bliss, is it?"

Humor rings in his words but it can't hide the malice underneath, reminding me this man is dangerous.

"You see, I work in a particular field. From what that idiot John told me, it seems your boyfriend has a side pet project of helping people, which really throws a wrench into my plan. The woman who came by, Diana, was it?" Does he mean Kelly? He has to, right? "Yes, she was a part of my operation, and when I found her missing, well... it's unacceptable."

The man struts like a peacock back to his desk.

"I sent Little John to go and retrieve her for me. Bring her back where she belongs. But it seems he was unable to do that. I doubt he tried very hard; the man has absolutely no intelligence. Really, I didn't have high expectations to begin with. No harm done. But seeing as I'm a woman down, I need someone to replace her.

"I have an auction coming up she was supposed to be a part of, and I can't afford the loss. I thought to have you take her place. But I think I have other plans for you now."

This man is bitter and angry, although at what or whom I don't know. Menacing is the only word to describe his expression. The measured tensing and relaxing of his hands hints at his need for violence. Vengeance.

"You look so much like her, you know. My wife, she left a few weeks ago on a trip with my son. They're not back yet and I've been worried about her, but I can't seem to locate her. I can't help but wonder if they're hiding out at that damn club."

Kneeling before me as he sneers, he takes my face firmly in his hand to the point of pain.

"So while she's away, I think a pretty stripper like you will do fine to keep me company."

The human body is really a miraculous thing. Its ability to protect the mind is a marvel.

I can sense my hunger and thirst. There are parts of my body that ache, but I know it isn't indicative of the full extent of whatever damage my body has endured. The miracle is that the only memories I have are from right before and right after. Those are the only moments I can't distance myself from.

I remember the knives. The cuts, scrapes, and deeper wounds he leaves. I remember the punches to my ribs and the sounds of cracking bone. The clink of a belt unbuckling and zipper being drawn. My mouth is involuntarily opened, and my jaw locks in place. My legs are forced to spread out, and my hips sting with pain from hands that hold me too harshly.

These are the only moments I can recall.

Time blurs in and out, and my consciousness only lasts for brief periods. It's impossible to tell whether I am dissociating, sleeping, or unconscious. I only have a cumulative sense of time from my more aware moments. There are no windows here. No way to keep track of the passing of time. But based on the dryness of my throat and hunger in my stomach, it must be days?

Hopes for rescue are pointless.

I resurface from the safe place in my mind to find myself chained in the middle of the room to one of the support beams. The man decided this would be part of his game. Me, trapped in the room with him, waiting for the violence I know is coming again.

Sometimes he looks up from whatever he is doing and smirks at me. As if seeing me like this brings him a sick form of pleasure. The memories of whatever he did to me turn him on. It's shortly after those moments I find myself back in the recesses of my mind.

I'm at camp. The river runs between the lush grounds surrounded by steep hills, and it sparkles as moonlight dances across its waters. There's faint music in the background. Melodies of campfire songs float towards me. There's an awareness that all of this isn't real, but I continue to live in the fantasy for as long as I can.

I hide in my dream because I don't know how much longer I can handle reality.

I have survived a lot in my life, but I've never truly broken before—until now.

I wish for an end. However it may come.

Even if it's my own ending.

VI

BE YOUR LOVE

Griffin

I've worked this job for over four years. A single guy recruited for an undercover assignment straight out of the police academy, I am needed here. Most importantly, I'm unattached. No one is left to worry about or miss me. I don't have anyone to worry about either. No partner or family to be missed. I reserve all of my time and mental energy for one central focus: my job.

My first assignment out of the academy thrust me into the world of sex trafficking and drugs working at the bottom of Arrick Mathieson's criminal enterprise. It's not a glamorous thing, but I adjusted quickly despite regularly witnessing the realities of this life.

I started as an underling distributing drugs for Arrick Mathieson's operation, which functions under the shell of Mathieson Enterprises. Over the years, I've worked my way up through the ranks. Now I stand in the boss' inner circle as head of security and can pass along vital information to the force about his habits and operations. Unfortunately, the man is paranoid. Of course, he's careful when it comes to his direct involvement. He distances himself so effectively we can never gather enough evidence to get him locked away.

Being so close to Arrick is an uncomfortable position. I know aiding the take-down of his drug and human trafficking operation will be worth it in the end, but morally I hate that I'm participating in such a cruel industry.

I've only just returned to the compound when one of the guys knocks on my door.

"Hey, boss wants to see you," he says.

I know the kid's face, but not his name. I think he's here because of a debt he owes?

"What about? I was gonna head over there later to report back. Why the urgency?"

Arrick's not normally like this. He's a planner. Everything is calculated. Why is he ignoring routines?

"Not sure. Either wants your report, or it's about what boss's got locked in his office."

That gets my attention. "What are you talking about?"

"Little John finally came through. Boss took an interest in what he brought back. I dunno man, I'm just the messenger."

I sigh. It's probably another woman.

Fuck.

"It's been great for the guys though. He's been a menace, but this chick seems to be doin' something for 'im."

His words confirm my fear. Arrick is unraveling fast. Since his family left, he's started spiraling out of control. I'm impressed though. For weeks I've been in and out of this hellhole looking for them. But there's nothing. They just disappeared.

"I'll head down."

The guy turns away and heads back to wherever he came from. I feel guilty about not knowing his name, unlike Higley who's been on our radar since he was in high school. But it's easier this way. It's simpler not to have attachments.

Immediately when I first see her, I feel this pull—a gravity I've never felt before, which has somehow suddenly attached itself to my soul. Galaxies are formed and destroyed when I first walk into the room. Her blonde hair falls over her shoulders and full lips peek out between the strands of gold. If you look past her wounds, you can see she's beautiful. With almost every inch of her skin on display I can clearly see every curve of her body. I'm drawn to her, and my world suddenly feels complete, but as quickly, the realization strikes me as to why she's here, and it's devastating.

Something so precious shouldn't be here. Not in a place like this. Not with people like him.

"Griffin," Arrick calls from across the room. His words sour the air. "Take care of this. I need it gone."

"Do you want an update on—" I'm cut off before I can finish.

"No. I don't want another fuckin' pointless update. You have nothing, do you?" His eyebrow raises. "Right, so go. And take her with you."

I admire her for a moment too long, and I guess Arrick takes it as indecision.

"Fuck her or kill her. I don't care. Get rid of her."

His words make bile rise up in my throat. I can't stomach looking at her injuries, and I can't ever imagine hurting her. Instincts demand I ensure her safety.

For fuck's sake, she's roped, and chains bind her to the room's central pier. Cuts mar her skin, and the bruises across her body are purple. I'm sure she's got a few broken bones, fractured ribs at the very least. There's cum caked in her hair; blood paints her body and embeds itself under her nails.

She fought back. At least for as long as she could. Good.

For a moment, my breath stops. Until I see the slightest rise and fall of her chest, that is. This fear is like nothing I've experienced before, and I've seen my fair share of violence and carnage. I know showing weakness in front of Arrick is not an option though.

I fix an unaffected mask on my face, a skill I was forced to learn very quickly here, and go about following his orders. Pushing gripping panic aside is the best way to protect her. It's the only thing I'm concerned with. I don't matter. Only her.

After freeing her from those chains, I place her over my shoulder, doing my best not to injure her more. Keeping her tied up grates at my core, but my protective compulsions overwrite my more tender feelings. I need her out of here more than anything.

I hear a smug cough from behind me.

"You don't have to carry her so delicately. She's worthless now."

His words haunt me as I make my way out the door and I barely stop the bile rising in my throat.

She's not worthless. She's mine.

As the distance between us and Arrick's torture chamber grows, I shift her into my arms. Her barely clothed and bound form is limp. Contentment builds in my chest with her in my arms, her face nestled in my chest. But, having her cradled where I can see her more clearly? Feel her?

Holding her like this is dangerous.

Whatever this connection is, it's going to get me killed.

Nothing matters but the woman cradled against my chest.

My treasure.

I make turns efficiently as I navigate my way through the grid of hallways. Reaching the corner stairwell door, I kick it open. Urgency thrums in my body, but I push it down. I make my way up to the top floor as quickly as possible without raising suspicions from anyone around. Let alone leave evidence on cameras, giving Arrick reason to question anything. I know the persistent feeling won't dissipate until I'm sure she's out of harms way. My entire body screams to get her out. Get her away. Make her safe.

It's the only thought running through my head, but I can't drop my guard yet. Arrick is a suspicious bastard and eerily omniscient at times. I know cameras are monitoring all the compound's entrances and exits. I don't doubt we're still being watched. My only option to avoid any kind of suspicion is to remain coldly guarded, at least until we're safely away from curious eyes.

My mind races with thoughts of how I can get her out, get her away. But I need a distraction to make that happen.

A big one.

When I reach the final hallway leading to my room, my steps slow, and my breathing begins to even out. I unlock the door to my room and shut us inside. Taking my first full breath only after the lock slides into place.

The room is sparse. Everything in the compound is built for Arrick's gang of soldiers, and he believes there is no comfort in this life. Our spaces reflect it. There are a few benefits to being trusted by him, however. Like having a nicer apartment-style space that feels less military base and more studio bachelor pad. But the emptiness is a constant reminder of how long it's been since I've had a normal life.

I debate setting her down on the bed, but looking at her broken body, I know I need to get her clean and bandaged. At least as much as I can. I can't stand the sight of his marks on her.

Taking her to the bathroom, I set her down on the floor leaning against the tub and move about, gathering what I will need. Washcloths, towels, antiseptic, bandages, something to wrap her ribs in.

I'm not a doctor or a medic of any kind, but the academy taught me enough. They make sure you know how to stitch up a wound and remove a bullet at least. The sight of blood is definitely not an issue either. I've ended enough people to block it out.

I delicately rearrange her in a chair I grab from the kitchen and position her head by the sink. It's a tight fit, and I'm forced to straddle her between my legs to reach the sink behind her. Our bodies are so close, and I can feel how cold she is.

I turn the water on and begin washing her hair. When I am done, I grab one of the washcloths to clean her. Lightly cupping her face, I start to wipe away the grime. Her eyes flutter a bit, and I feel her relax at my touch. The satisfaction blooming through me at this display of trust is incomparable.

When I finish cleaning her face and neck, I start to remove my hands, but her cheek follows my touch as I do.

Even like this, she's beautiful.

With her hair clean and wet, you can see it isn't pure blonde. There are hidden shades of rust amongst the gold framing her striking face. Her eyes are closed, but I'm curious to know what color they are. You can tell this woman knows joy and laughter and love by the lines around her eyes.

It's heartbreaking.

I can't imagine what she's experienced in the days she spent in Arrick's office. I was away on assignment, doing a poor job of looking for Sage and Kieran. But guilt still eats at me, knowing how she must have suffered. And that I might have been able to do something.

I've never believed in love at first sight before, but I do now.

I know I can easily devote my life to this woman. I'll do anything to give her the world. To even be a part of her life will be a privilege.

Withdrawing, I continue to clean her body. Despite her condition, I can't help but admire her curves, the stretch marks on her stomach and thighs. Though bruises and deep wounds cover her, I adore the paleness of her skin and the rose returning to her cheeks as she begins to warm up.

I hesitate at removing her remaining undergarments. But it seems better to remove the filthy pieces rather than leave her in discomfort.

I complete cleaning her and after my crude attempt at playing doctor, I cross to my dresser to find the softest clothing I own: my gray sweatpants, black T-shirt, and warm wool socks.

Taking her into my arms, I wrap her own around my neck. I nearly stumble when I feel them tighten around me. My head bends down towards her, and I feel deep pleasure when I smell her wrapped in my own scent.

I walk her over to my bed and lay her down. She takes up the whole thing, but it doesn't stop my desire to climb in with her; my craving to lie there holding her. Ignoring the thought, I tuck her into the warmth and lay another blanket across her.

Everything in my body screams that my life's purpose is to care for this woman. More than my promise to protect and serve or any other vow I've made.

It starts now, and I won't let myself fail her.

STRESSED

Jay

As far as nightmares go, this one's the worst. Because this is real. I'm living it.

My best friend is gone.

Fucking kidnapped by some white man with the audacity.

After seeing what he did on the security cameras, Rosie and I call the police. Rosie usually is so calm and personable. That night, she lost it. I don't think I've ever seen her talk quite so fast or get so frustrated with anyone. Hell, this is a woman who manages to stay polite on the phone with the cable company. But that night, all patience is gone. The 911 operator must have asked her to slow down or repeat herself six times. Which is absolutely not helping the situation.

There were cops and techs everywhere. Rosie and I gave our statements to the uniforms who initially arrived on the scene. Another pair came shortly after who must be their superiors. Detective Wright and Detective Bacon took our statements again. Thankfully, our statements are recorded.

To be questioned by the police like this is an odd feeling. Even the surface-level questions are invasive, and they became increasingly more so as we talk. They dissected my life as if that's where the answer for her disappearance lies. Even with the video evidence showing exactly who took her. As if I could have possibly had something to do with it. As if I would ever hurt Julia.

The person I care about most in this world is in danger, possibly hurt or worse, and here the police are questioning me like I'm the problem. Logically, I never genuinely think they are trying to accuse me of anything. Still, it feels wrong to be so vulnerable with people I don't know.

Bringing in the police gives me fleeting hope. But once they left, everything grinds to a halt, and there is nothing to suppress the feelings of dread popping up again and again. I call to speak with the detective every day after Julia's taken. I know this isn't their only case, but I need something from them. I'm falling apart without something to occupy me. Without Julia, life dims, and I'm merely going through the motions.

Of course, the detectives are busy or out of the office when I call, which doesn't help any with the urgency I feel. I need them to feel it too. I need them to have the air sucked from their lungs. To experience time standing still while everyone keeps moving, and no matter how loud they scream, no one stops.

No matter how many people tell me, I can't get past the feeling this was somehow my fault. I feel helpless, useless. All while knowing I'm a failure. Not only that. But I've failed *her*.

I run through the events of the day a thousand times.

I should have known when Kelly showed up. Julia wasn't out on the floor like she typically was when the club opened because of that meeting. I should have known, right?

When things escalated on the floor with Chad, I should have sensed it would lead to problems. I should have never left her alone at the club. I should have waited for her, stayed. I should have gone with her. I should have watched her get in her car. I should have driven her home.

I should have.

Should. Should. Should.

The word pounds in my skull. It's a judgment, sure. Should's are only ever that. A judgment we press upon ourselves. But it's so fitting, so right, to blame myself. The judgments don't stop running through my mind. I'm the only one deserving of criticism and guilt.

I know this is one of those chaos-of-the-universe situations. It's not something that could have been avoided with careful planning and safety procedures. I couldn't have predicted any of this. Sometimes things just happen. But that isn't a satisfying answer.

My thoughts circle back to the list of should's that, ironically, should have happened.

I'm sitting in Julia's office when Rosie walks in. She looks at me with pity and regret. But the emotion seems misplaced on her features. What on earth could she regret? Rosie isn't a woman who regrets anything. She didn't do anything.

But neither did I. That's the problem.

It's me who could have done something to avoid all of this. If it weren't for me, then Julia would still be here. Safe and sound with her family. With me.

"Jay Bird. You need to stop this."

"I don't know what you're talking about." I brush her off, saying, "I'm fine."

"No, you're not, birdie. You're a mess and have been all week. The staff is uneasy with your mood swings. No one knows how to act around you." She sighs, and I know she's right, but I don't want to face everything. It's easier to hide behind my guilt.

"Look, I get it. I can only begin to imagine how much you are hurting. But you're not the only person who loved her, okay? We all miss her. We all want her back," she continues.

"Loved? Already switching to past tense, are we?

Like she's already gone and not coming back."

"Fuck, Jay. You know what I mean. Stop being a dick about my fucking verb tense."

I'm too on edge to respond. I know she's right. I owe so many people apologies for how I'm acting. Without Julia, I'm the worst version of myself. This isn't going away either. It only seems to worsen every day she's not here.

The police haven't made any progress, and it's driving me up a wall. We have fucking video evidence of the man taking her. But they still aren't able to identify who it is. Because of course, "Chad" is fictional.

Kelly knows nothing. The police questioned her until I had to drag her out crying. She never said anything useful. Even when I spoke with her about it later, the only details she shared with me were that she didn't actually know him well but thought his name was John. Not that it's entirely unusual for victims. Some people need to share, and others need to keep things to themselves until they can process the memories. Until they sort them into more manageable pieces.

The most frustrating part of the process is knowing Julia could be in pain. I'm helpless to do anything. Every morning I wake up dreading what the day may bring. It will either be good or terrible news. There is no in-between.

Only when she's found safe will I be able to breathe.

But every day passing where they have no new information is pure torture.

The lines between right and wrong are starting to blur as life goes on without her. The taste of iron in my mouth reminds me how, given the chance, I would love to see John bloodied beyond recognition.

The thought of that kind of violence only makes the tightness in my chest worsen. The possibility of someone harming Julia is not an image I want to conjure. The bastard stabbed her with a syringe to take her away. Who knows what he and his buddies will do to her if that's the escalation they are willing to take to obtain a person? Because surely this man is not smart enough to be working alone.

"Jay, you're not listening, are you?"

"Sorry."

"No, you're really not." Rosie exhales, and I can see her eyes narrow as she thinks through something. "We're worried about you. The police are doing everything they can, and you check in with them every day. You're hyper-focused on keeping the club running for her, and Julia would be thankful for you taking care of everyone. But you're kind of falling apart, and it's starting to scare the staff. I'm worried about you too, and I don't want to see you continue like this. She wouldn't want this for you."

I know she's right. I am starting to scare myself, if

I'm being honest. Even Julia's dog, Spencer, has been nervous around me since I brought him back to my place. The most lovable and chill dog I've ever met is scared of me. It's an awful feeling.

One more to add to all of the others.

Nothing makes sense anymore. My whole world is off its axis without her, and I'm not sure how to right myself. Shame and guilt roar in my ear day and night, threatening to consume me. I need to do something. Anything to feel like I'm making progress. Anything to assure me I will get her back.

Hours later, I'm on the floor, and my phone vibrates in my pocket. I pull it out to see an unknown number. My feet are already moving, and I give Rosie a silent nod, gesturing to the office.

"Jay Maddox."

"Hi, Jay. This is Detective Bacon calling about your friend's case."

"Oh. Detective." I hold in my laugh. Despite the difficulties of this week, I will never get over this woman's name. It makes me chuckle every time. "Do you have any information? Have you found her?"

"We still haven't been able to locate her. I'm sorry." I know it's coming, but the statement hurts nonetheless. "However," she says, and my heart picks up, "your friend Kelly was more helpful than we originally thought. We've been able to identify the man that took her. Do you know John Higley by any chance? Goes by Little John?"

My prayers are answered for once.

"Never heard of him before." I hesitate to confirm. "He was the guy who took her?"

"It appears so. We haven't been able to locate him to make an arrest." The detective pauses. "I'm not supposed to tell you, but we suspect that he's connected to Mathieson Enterprises. I wouldn't be surprised if this was somehow involved."

The detective's tone belies only honest and genuine concern. She doesn't sound like someone who twists words or information. But people are by nature selfish and manipulative.

Except for Julia. Except for the one woman I know who pours every piece of herself into those around her. Except the person who drops everything for a friend.

The realization hits me after a moment. I have a name.

When Kelly finally told us the man's name was John, Rosie worked through her network best she could to find out his identity, but we came up empty. I was powerless to do anything for those weeks because I didn't know anything. But now, I'm armed with the man's name. We can lean on Rosie's friends, shady or not, to find this asshole and press him to the edge until I get what I need from him. I don't have to follow the straight and narrow anymore; I have options.

I'm not typically a violent person. But for Julia, I'll be anything she needs. Right now, she needs someone to hunt down her enemies. Someone to free her from whatever hell she's being held captive in.

"Detective, I have to go."

"Oh, okay. I do have a few more questions for you. When you have time, please call—"

I don't allow her to finish before I end the call. I'm already moving to find Rosie. Probably our head of security, Gus, too. They will know what to do with the name.

I will find him, and then I will find her. I have to.

BLUE EYES BLIND

Juliana

I feel a presence, but there's no way to tell who it is.

All I know is I'm being cared for. I'm gently given sips of water, and at one point, my body is repositioned because I'm still too weak to do it on my own.

None of this makes sense.

I've spent days being degraded, violated, and tortured. Any rest I have is fitful and unsettling. My body needs rest to heal, but it remains hypervigilant. Not that I can do anything to protect myself should I face a threat.

When I do manage sleep, I hear a voice somewhere in the distance. The muffled murmurs are comforting even if I don't understand the words. Sometimes the fuzzy words are directed at me. Sometimes it speaks about nothing at all. Regardless, there's tenderness there.

Touch is the second sensation to come back to me. Unfortunately, it comes with a nasty partner in crime—

pain. My jaw hurts and muscles scream. My ribs ache every time I move, the bruises settling deep in my marrow. It stings and itches near every incision on my skin. Everything is pain.

Occasionally, I feel a soft touch on my forehead or cheek. Something skims my arm and lingers at my wrist. The touch is so tender, so careful and sweet. In contrast with the physical damage my body endured, it feels like ecstasy. There's no better escape than the caresses I feel, and I crave them more with each hour that passes.

The contact and care slowly bring me back to consciousness. The voice speaks for a while, and the words become clearer. It's seductive. It's safe. The more I listen, the more I need to know who it belongs to.

I gather what energy I have and peel back the curtain of my eyelids to take in my surroundings. My first impression has me on edge. It looks too similar to the room I was held captive in. The exposed metal beams and stained concrete floors are the same. Even the wood furniture looks similar. Like it was all bought in bulk at once to fill a dorm building.

I start to doubt the pleasant memories from my slumber. Surely, I'm still chained to that support beam, covered in filth, silently begging for an ending I know will come.

Upon further observation, I discover this is a different space altogether. Some windows let in natural light, and I'm positioned in a bed, not on the floor. The tightness around my ribs and soft fabric that cocoons me tell me someone has cleaned, bandaged, and dressed me too.

Goddess, something smells good. I turn my head to gather more of the scent. The sheets smell like cloves. And lemon?

I can't help but continue to turn my body into the comfort of the scent. It's like Christmas and spring cleaning together. Both winter and summer. I sink into the duality.

My eyes close briefly, and I hear a shuffling noise across the room. I'm on high alert as my head jerks toward the sound.

I must look awful since the man immediately stops. His demeanor is warm but calculated. It's like he's trying to anticipate and measure my reactions. The patience of this man would have driven me mad under normal circumstances. But I no longer live in normal circumstances.

I take his quiet stillness as a gift. He gives me a moment to decide what I want without pressure or influence.

I nod, giving him permission to approach. He does so slowly so I can track his movements. He's acting as though I'm a skittish animal, which I guess I am.

"Hi." His voice is so familiar. "You're awake. Good."

I stay silent. There is no way to tell his motivations, and I don't want to risk placing myself in a situation where I'm set up to face another man's outrage.

Settling on his knees before me as I lie in what I'm assuming is his bed, the look in his eyes speaks to pure relief and adoration. It's bizarre to see such unadulterated emotion come from a stranger, much less such a masculine-looking man. Before I can examine the moment of vulnerability further, his face blanks to a neutral expression.

It feels right to see him on his knees. To see him tilting up his face to me, looking for permission. I am powerless here and entirely at his mercy, as cliché as it sounds. Yet he defers to me.

"I've been worrying about you. It's been a week since I brought you up here." His hand reaches out as if he wants to touch me, but retreats as he thinks better of the action. "Sorry. I shouldn't do that."

I study the man. A break in his nose grounds features that might otherwise be almost too pretty. His lips are pressed together, and I long to see his full smile. His inky hair looks soft to the touch, and my fingers ache to run through it. To grab it by the roots and pull. Warm features make his face open up as he looks at me with mesmerizing ocher eyes; a girl could get lost in those eyes.

My gaze slides down his face, and I study his body like an artist. Tanned skin contrasts the dark tattoos running down his neck and into his long-sleeved shirt where they peek out from under the cuffs on his strong hands. The image of stripping off his clothes to touch every stroke the artist left on his skin floats through my mind, sending a shiver down my spine.

"Oh, are you cold?" He stands to move away and grabs a blanket from the foot of the bed. "Here."

He tucks me into the blanket, literally tucks, and lowers himself to his knees. Like it's the most natural thing in the world, his hands wait on his knees, and my breath is stolen once more when he glances down for a moment, refusing to meet my eyes.

I like seeing him there.

His hand reaches out as though to touch me, and I flinch involuntarily. My body reacts before my brain can come up with a reason for the action.

This man isn't a threat. I know it, but my body doesn't know better.

Like he can read my mind, he slows his movement this time. When I feel the warm tips of his fingers against my face, moving the hair in my eyes behind my ear, I shiver again. This man's touch is intoxicating, and I'm growing addicted to the feeling of tension escaping my body at his nearness.

It's him.

It must be him.

The voice I heard. The touch I felt while I was recovering. The presence who brought back my sense of peace. Despite everything, a part of me feels safe with this man. He must be the presence I have become so attuned to over the past few days.

There is no sense to it, but the feeling that he is essential confronts me. Something in my soul says I should embrace this man and what he offers; his protection and care.

"I'm Griffin. Do you have a name?" He laughs a little at himself. "Well, of course you do. Sorry. I'm gonna start over. My name is Griffin, or Griff to those who like me. What's yours?"

It's such a formal introduction, yet still so genuine. I would have laughed if I the energy.

"You know what? Doesn't matter." His face is soft and relaxed. His fingers haven't left my skin, though they've traveled to trace circles at my wrist with a feather touch. We share a comfortable moment of quiet like ones between couples who have been together forever. Where simply being in the other's presence is a comfort. "Wanna sit up?"

I merely nod at the suggestion. If I'm being honest, I want his hands to stay on me. You would think I would continue to recoil at his touch, but it's almost like the only time my body relaxes is when he's touching me. My body craves this man. I need him.

His arm reaches beneath me and pulls me up to his chest, and the blanket that encompassed me falls down. My hands automatically move to rest on the defined muscle there. He grabs some extra pillows and stacks them behind me. Though he tries to set me back to rest, my hands search for his neck. I don't want to let go.

He pulls his head back a little to look at me with curiosity. I see the question there but don't know how to respond. Neither of us move to release the embrace. But the moment grows awkward soon enough.

A cough escapes my throat.

"How about I grab you a glass of water?" he asks.

It doesn't look like he really wants to leave, but his suggestion gives us both an easy out rather than dealing with whatever is building between us.

The man, Griffin, moves to the kitchen. Opening a cabinet and then the fridge, I hear him pour. Some extra rustling makes my head turn. He walks back over with the water and a parchment bag.

"Here you go," he says, handing me a glass. "If you're up for it, I grabbed chocolate croissants from the bakery around the corner this morning."

It's such a sweet gesture. I regret having to shake my head at him.

"What, not a sweets person?"

Shaking my head, I think about how to best explain. Finally, I motion to my throat and make a clenching gesture with my fist.

He looks puzzled for a moment, but then it seems to dawn on him. "Oh, are you allergic? Like you can't breathe because of it?"

"Gluten." I manage to summon my voice back for this.

The elation that comes over his face at one simple word could power a small city. I have no idea how much I'm capable of speaking, but his reaction is worth every effort.

What a stupid first thing to say to this man.

Stupid voice.

Stupid food allergies.

During my week of captivity, I almost wished they did feed me something. That way, there was a chance of having a fatal anaphylactic reaction. It would have been preferable to everything I endured, remembered or not.

I hear him chuckle. I love the sound. It's rumbly and warm, and it brings levity to the room.

"Okay, well, we will have to get more details out of you about that later, but I do want you to eat something. Do you think you could get a smoothie down?"

It's sweet of him to go to such lengths for me, and the earnest look on his face decides it. I really am hungry. Something about Griffin's eager look makes me agree.

Back in the kitchen, I can hear him moving about. I sit there sipping on my water and staring out the window while he rustles around. Then he's back at my side with a container.

"Anything in here you can't eat? Nothin's gonna harm you?"

I realize he wants me to read the nutrition label. I glance over it before responding.

"No," I say, smiling as much as I can.

"Perfect. It's a protein powder, which you could probably use. Are fruits okay?"

I nod.

He's still smiling when he turns around this time. He's like a puppy. Eager to please.

I tune out the sounds coming from the kitchen and study the room I'm in. It appears to be a studio apartment with the living room in front of me. No TV though. A few books are stacked on the coffee table. The bathroom is to my left, and the kitchen is behind a wall where a few photos hang.

Looking around, there doesn't seem to be a single personal item about. Everything is simple and stream-lined. The few things here are either necessities or what feels like set dressing. None are personal; they're pictures of sports icons and other generic items.

Griffin appears with another glass in his hand.

For the third time since I've awakened, he kneels beside me. Reaching out, he motions for the drink in my hand, which I release tentatively before he hands me the chilled smoothie glass. Then he turns his full attention back to me.

Goddess, he's attractive.

"So, do you think you can try and tell me your name?"

I think about lying to him for a moment, but the thought disappears faster than it formed.

"Juliana."

RESCUE

Griffin

*J*uliana.

It's embarrassing to admit but having her tell me her name is the most rewarding experience. More than graduating from college, the academy, or any other accomplishment so far in life. It feels like I've been gifted with something precious.

Growing up, a German family in our apartment complex gave us a leather-bound book with all of the fairy tales. It was a Christmas present, and Abuela, never one to dismiss the kindness of others, read the stories to me every single night. She did it both to practice her English and also to spend time with me and my sister. Those nights reading are some of my favorite memories with her.

There was one story about faeries who collected the names that became my favorite. After hearing the story a hundred times, I developed a similar superstition about the important nature of names. Living for years as a man who doesn't really exist for this assignment only reinforces the idea. Names are a person's identity in so many ways. So knowing this woman's name, a person I already count as part of my soul, is like being gifted breath itself.

It feels good to have Juliana's gaze on me, her complete focus. The way she holds no fear in her eyes calms me.

She has captivating indigo eyes. They sparkle like geodes, and their color deepens as you gaze further into them. Her laugh lines are beautiful, and I want to see that expression on her face, to witness her unfiltered happiness. I want to be the person who does that for her. I want to bring her joy.

"Well then, Juliana, it's lovely to meet you."

Not knowing what to do next, I stand abruptly. She looks up at me a little startled. But before I'm able to move away, she surprises me by patting the bed. She wants me to sit with her?

After everything, it makes no sense for her to be so relaxed around me. For her to want to be near me seems counterintuitive. It's surprising but no less satisfying.

In the academy, I saw victims and heard stories from the veteran officers about how survivors of violence, especially sexual violence, react afterward. But her face is still trusting, and she looks at me as though

I am a longtime friend who came over to visit.

No way in heaven or hell will I pass up this moment.

I move tentatively to her side. She places the straw between her plump lips, and I want to kiss her. Possess her. Protect her. But I suppress the instinct to take what I want, no matter how normal she appears. She's gone through things no one should have to live through. The wounds I've cared for are evidence of that. So I'll be as patient as she needs. My own desires are secondary to anything she needs. I can't afford to frighten her or push her away. If I do, I may never gain that trust again.

That kind of loss would crush me.

We sit quietly while she drinks, and she looks around before speaking.

"Why are there no pictures?" Her voice is returning. It's melodic and seductive with a slightly raspy quality. It only adds to her allure.

It's not what I was expecting at all. I would think she would want to know where she is or when she can leave. Instead, she's asking me about pictures? I look around the room, trying to see as she does.

"You have some of athletes, I guess? But nothing personal."

"Oh, yeah. Well, um... I don't live here all the time. That's part of it. But also, I don't want to leave a whole lot of evidence around that I was here," I explain. "Wait, do you not know who Craig Biggio is? Altuve?"

Cheeks flush with embarrassment, she redirects. "Evidence?"

Well, I guess this is as good a way to tell her as any.

"Yeah. Um…" I think about how best to tell her. Out of habit, my hand goes to the back of my neck, and I tug at my hair slightly. A curious fire sparks in her face in response. "Look, I can't tell you a whole lot yet. I need you to trust me, okay?"

"Oh, okay," is her only response.

Confused by her reaction, I press on. "You're at the headquarters of Mathieson Enterprises. It's a compound of sorts. I live here most of the time."

"Okay."

"I'm sure you have questions," I say, thinking maybe a prompt would get her to open up.

"Probably, but not yet." The way her words feather over me nearly makes me groan. But she's acting oddly, and I can't figure out why.

"Look, I want to get you out. This isn't a place you want to be."

"Why don't we leave then?" she asks, wide-eyed.

"I have to sort out a couple things first. Okay? I'm head of security here. I can't just disappear." I pause to prepare myself. "I can't risk something happening to you. We need a plan." Her silence is telling. She doesn't like this, but I appreciate that she doesn't question me. "I'm going to leave for a bit. Do you have everything you need? I should only be gone for a few hours."

Her answer is simple. "I'm good."

"Okay. Don't leave the room, alright? I need you to stay here. You're safe in here, but I do need to lock you in..." It's all I want, but I refrain from touching her. "By the way, what's your last name?"

"Morgan, Juliana Morgan."

I give her my first smile in months. "Okay, good. Juliana Morgan," I repeat, tucking away the information. "Yeah, I'm leaving now. Okay?"

But I can't manage to move.

"Bye, Griffin," she prompts. But her smile makes me want to stay.

I leave anyway. For her.

I have to school my smile away as I leave to avoid suspicious gazes. But once I'm far enough away, I make a call.

They pick up on the first ring.

"Meet me at the normal spot," I say.

"I can be there in fifteen minutes."

"I'll see you in thirty." I hang up, put the car in drive, and head to the meeting spot.

Arriving at the George R. Brown Convention Center, I see it's packed like I'd hoped. It looks like a Comic-Con or something with how everyone is dressed up. The inability to see anyone for who they really are in cos-play is terrifying; it's like mascots. Can't trust 'em.

Pushing through the throngs of people, I make my way to the welcome desk. I keep an eye out for anyone following me as I approach, but it feels safer with so many people about. Finally, I see the sign, and beneath it, my friend, Detective Quinn Emmerson.

"Hey, I'm hoping you can help me. I've lost my phone. Do you have a lost and found here?" I say.

"Of course. Let's go in the back and take a look."

We make our way into a small storage room, and he waits until the door is shut and locked before speaking.

"Lost and found? That's a new one," he jokes.

"Yeah, well, it's fitting, considering. Look, I don't have time for pleasantries."

"Fill me in."

I try to get through all the relevant information as quickly as possible. I don't want to take any longer than I need to get back to my Jules.

"There's a girl you need help extracting." Exhaustion takes over his features. "Dude, I know you've seen a lot, but I gotta ask, why her? You know we still don't have enough to take Mathieson down. You know you're going to blow up four years of work, right? We still don't know how the other girls got out. It's shitty for sure, but I'm gonna need a damn good reason to convince the brass we need to do this for one girl.”

Shame pops up at the mention of the other girls I secretly helped. Then guilt because I know I can't take the same risk for Jules so close to the last girl without raising Arrick's suspicions.

“He's unraveling fast. Arrick's wife left with their son a month ago, and he sent me out a week ago to try and track her down.” I can't exactly tell him the real reason they left or how. “When I got back, I was called into his office. This girl was chained to a beam. I was told to 'take care of it.' She's not in good shape; I'm worried about what happens if she stays.”

“Shit, you care about her.”

“Yes,” I share quietly. It feels like a personal thing to admit, but I know Quinn will step up if he knows.

“You've known her for what, a few days?”

“Does it really matter? She's injured. Badly. And completely innocent in all of this.”

“Fuck. Okay, what's the girl's name? I'll see what I can do.” He pulls out his pocket notebook.

“Juliana Morgan.”

“Well, fuck. Fuck. Fuck. Fuck. Fuck. Fuck,” he chants. “Hold on, I need to make a call.”

Pulling out his phone, he dials and puts it on speaker.

“Detective Bacon speaking.”

“Gracie, hey, it's Quinn. Are you still working on the

Bliss kidnapping case?"

This is not good.

"Yeah, and it's a pain in the ass. A friend of hers calls every day looking for an update. I have nothing to give him. Still calls back like clockwork though. Honestly, the lieutenant is pushing me to drop the case already, and it's only been two weeks."

"I might be able to help you out with that one."

"What are you talking about?"

"You know the Mathieson case? Drugs. Trafficking. Well, I was talking with my guy, and he says a girl came through. Name sounded familiar, so I called you."

"I'm on the edge of my seat."

"Any chance your girl is named Juliana Morgan?"

"Shit." She sighs over the phone, and we hear the rustling of papers. "Is he with you?"

"Yeah."

"Hold on. I'm pulling up her info so he can verify."

We wait in silence while more rustling and typing noises come over the phone.

"Okay. Juliana 'Julia' Morgan. Blonde. Blue eyes. Five-foot-nine. I'm guessing this 180 pounds on her license isn't right anymore based on the friend's description. Sound like her?"

I nod in affirmation.

"Yeah, that's her," my friend says.

"Shit. If she's involved in your case... It complicates

things. A lot."

Complicated indeed.

"Look, get back here, and we can talk with the higher-up's to see what can be done. I guess I finally get to give the friend good news though. Speak of the devil." She sighs. "I gotta go."

The detective hangs up, and we stare at each other.

"Looks like you might get your miracle, bud," he says.

"Maybe."

No matter how much I try, I can't help the hope and relief building in my chest. If they get the okay, I can get her out somewhere safe. I won't have to worry about her anymore. Her problems would be off my plate.

But do I really want that? I don't think so. There's a corner of my mind that has already started to imagine what life would be like if I followed her.

I'll be okay with whatever plan they come up with. I have to be.

As long as she's safe.

KILL OF THE NIGHT

I've never seen the underbelly of the city before, but this is important. More than that, it's necessary. Finding the man who took Julia feels like the only thing keeping me going at this point.

With a name from the detective in hand, I search for Rosie. She somehow knows everyone. As expected, Rosie knows a person who knows a girl who dates a guy that can help us track down John Higley. It's through this network of somewhat shady characters we finally locate him.

I swear I'll never question her, and when we get Julia back, Rosie is getting a raise. And a promotion.

I've been slowly dying over the past weeks without Julia. The good memories are becoming harder to recall, and the darkness is closing in. How long before I forget her face? Her voice? You hear about it happening when you lose someone. It's like all the light is sucked out of my life. I'm only left with my darkest thoughts.

I've never been violent, but there's always one thing that will drive a person to their limit and push them over. When I think about it, at this point there is nothing I wouldn't do to have Julia back safely.

This man, he took from me. He did this, and he will suffer for his actions.

I don't know when I decided this was the route I would take. Instead, it feels like there's only one path forward. When the most vital person in your life is taken, there's no line you won't cross. I'm sure for some people there is, but for me, the moment I saw him on the security tapes with his hand around Julia's throat, it disappeared.

I need this man to experience violence at my hands.

Inexperienced as we are, Rosie and I decided to hire help from professionals. We need them to help us obtain the target, who would then be taken to a more remote location. Namely, a remote piece of land owned by a ghost outside the city. We are instructed to wait for a call confirming delivery. Then we will be given instructions on where to go.

Really, it's quite an efficient business model they have going for them. You pay them, whomever they may be, an absurd amount of money. Then they arrange every detail a person needs for their revenge. The whole process even includes a questionnaire to know which supplies they should stock. It seems some people can be very particular about their tools. It's an impressive level of attention to detail. Who knew the underworld could be so organized?

There's no reason for my involvement in tracking him down, but I can't keep myself away. I took the information Rosie was given about Higley and found him at a bar in The Heights getting drunk with buddies and hitting on women who clearly don't want his attention. The man is my only connection to Julia, and I want to see his face when the tables are finally turned against him. I want to witness when he realizes how fucked he is.

He's stumbling out of the bar with a bouncer close behind him.

"Go home. You're drunk." The bouncer gives Higley a last shove out the door.

I'm following quietly behind as Higley stumbles along the sidewalk before collapsing on the corner.

I can't think about the idea of Julia not coming home, but the more time that passes, the more likely it becomes. I can't let this drag on any longer. This needs to end, *he* needs to end.

I'm looking around, slightly panicked, wondering where they are. I can't help but think the plan's gone wrong. We've missed our opportunity, and the man is going to get a ride home after another night of drinking. I see a cab pull up to the curb, and my stomach drops.

Houston doesn't have cabs driving around waiting for passengers.

My pulse picks up as I realize who must be getting out of the cab. They make their way over to the drunken man sprawled on the corner and haul him to the back seat of the car. Then the driver goes around the car, ripping off decals and quickly replacing the license plates with new ones. The movement is practiced and efficient. Soon, the cab is transformed into a nondescript rideshare.

The urgency I feel diminishes a bit knowing the man I loathe is on his way to his end, and I turn to head back to my own truck.

I spend the rest of the evening pacing in Julia's office, waiting for the phone call. At some point, someone drops food off for me, and Rosie even tries to get me to have a drink, but I can't stomach it.

I'm not apprehensive about what I plan to do to this man. No matter how dark and gruesome the desires are. No, if anything, making this commitment is the easy part. Instead, I'm hung up on the fact he may not know enough to help us, or what he does tell us might not help us find her. Plus, while Rosie is highly committed to the endeavor, I worry the level of violence simmering in me might be too much for her to witness.

Rosie's head pops in before she even knocks.

"Hey, there." She looks like she's bracing herself.

All day, she's been poking her head in and out of the office, and it's grating on my nerves. I'm short-tempered and snappy. She's tried flirting and joking and scolding me, but nothing is going to get my mind off of what's happening tonight. It makes sense that she's on edge as well with how I've been acting out. I'm not making things easy for her.

"Hey," I grumble back, trying to stretch my patience.

"I see you're still on a hunger strike here."

I want to lash out at her, but she doesn't deserve it. She deserves so much better from me. Without Rosie, I wouldn't have made it this far. I would have fallen to pieces days ago.

"I can't."

Stepping through, she shuts the door behind her and comes to stand behind the chairs in front of Julia's desk.

"Still waiting?"

"Yeah."

"It will come. But in the meantime, try to eat something."

My indifferent shrug earns me a silent reprimand.

"Can I wait with you?" She makes her way to the plush chair across from me and sits. We wait for the call to come in silence.

My whole body is vibrating in anticipation. Knowing you're able to take action and taking those steps are two very different things. My body knows the difference. With the first, I'm on edge, and everything still feels out of control. But the second momentum starts, the anxiety falls away. The initial push is the hardest part. Inertia and all that.

When the phone rings, my whole world stands still. I reach for it.

It's a blocked number.

Rosie looks at me meaningfully as I answer.

"Hello?"

As expected, the address they provide is outside the city in the middle of nowhere. We immediately jump into the provided unmarked car and drive for what feels like hours. Though it surely can't be since we haven't passed a Buc-ee's yet.

Driving through the wilderness and dirt roads of Texas is different than you would imagine. Everything is so flat it doesn't feel ominous in the way a thick forest might. Instead, you can see for such a distance in the dim moonlight, and everything feels massive. You start to feel so small and insignificant. The sheer scale of everything makes it terrifying.

Driving towards a dilapidated barn in the middle of nowhere doesn't help with the unease I feel.

"Rosie, you don't have to be here if you don't want to. I can do this myself. You can stay in the car. Or better yet, leave. I'll drive you back even," I say.

"Jay Bird, she's my friend too. I'm good right here."

"Okay, but you know this isn't going to be pretty."

An unfortunate truth. But from the little we learned about John Higley from the police report Rosie got her hands on by flirting with a cop who came into the club, it seems the man never made a good decision in his young life. Everything he's involved in has at least a few shady characters or dealings attached. He has several arrests. Yet before he's dragged into a courtroom, everything disappears. Never a good sign.

A part of me is scared of what might happen next. Anyone would be an idiot not to be a little scared. But mostly I am afraid of how this will change me. Will it change how Julia sees me? Will she love me if she learns the lengths I will go to for her?

These are the questions haunting me as Rosie and I get out of the car.

The barn is dimly lit with only a few flickering bulbs. Walking farther in, we finally see him. He's tied up and slumped over in a chair underneath a single light, looking a little worse for wear than when I'd seen him outside the bar. Looks like someone already roughed him up a bit. I guess Rosie's new friends felt the need to help us out. A courtesy, really.

I look around the room and take in the space around us, noticing the complete set of tools off to the side. My fingers twitch eagerly. Walking over, my eyes widen as I take in each piece lying on the table.

Evidently, our questionnaire told them we needed everything under the sun.

Sure, I have no experience in this kind of thing. Even without it, there's a deeply buried and long unacknowledged part of me that craves the violence and bloodshed that awaits. I pick up a pair of pliers, and calm settles upon me. It feels right to be holding these. To be here for this specific task.

"Rosie, is there a bucket anywhere?"

"Not sure. I'll look around."

"If you find one, fill it up with water."

I look down at the pliers in my hand, and a peace settles over me. I'm not doing this for myself, but I relish how capable I feel with these tools.

Turning on my boot heel, I face a soon-to-be dead man.

Despite the urgency driving me, my approach is slow. I am more aware of my surroundings, the sounds, and the movements all around us. The rise and fall of his chest put me in a rage.

I want this man dead.

Rosie comes back with a bucket filled with water, but there is a mischievous glint in her eyes. She looks like she's enjoying herself.

"Would you like to do the honors, or shall I?" Amusement lights her face.

"Have at it."

I step back to avoid the splash of water as she chucks it and the bucket itself at our unconscious friend, who starts awake.

Nothing like the crash of reality to wake a person up.

His head swivels back and forth slightly while he tries to take in the room around him. When his miserable circumstance finally dawns on him, he bolts upright.

"What the hell. Where am I?"

"Well, you got it right the first time." The words spill out of my mouth before I can think them through, but it feels good to be on the offensive. "For you, this will be your intro to hell. But I'm sure you'll make your way to the real thing very soon."

Clearly, my words affect him. His eyes widen as he

realizes who I am.

"You…"

"Yes. Me," I reply. "You took something of mine, and I want it back. So here's the deal. Either you make this easy for yourself and tell us where to find her, or we use the tools over on the table until you do."

His eyes connect with the pliers in my hand before he turns to gaze at the table. I note which tools make the man's eyes widen in fear as he takes in the array of implements.

"Well?" Waiting will not do this man any favors.

"Look, you really don't need to hurt me. I'll tell you whatever you want to know."

I look over at Rosie. Her face hasn't changed at all. The subtle shift in her eyes to me says his response is not what either of us expected.

"Okay, and what is it you have to tell us?" I ask.

"Your friend, right? The hot bimbo that was hanging off of you at the club? You want to know where she is, right?"

Shit. He really will tell us what we want to know, won't he?

It's then I smell the acidic scent of piss and witness tears stream down his face.

What a fucking coward. He deserves to die. No matter how cooperative he is in the end.

"Look, I got involved with bad people and needed

an out. Boss said I could walk away if I got his merchandise back for him and figured out what was going on at your club."

My eyebrows raise as a silent prompt. His boss is probably lying to him.

"I came looking at your place for the girl. I couldn't come back with nothing when I couldn't find the bitch. I took your girlfriend instead." He is panting hard, with a very satisfying panic resonating in his voice.

What on earth?

"Do you mean the merchandise you were supposed to take back with you was a woman? The woman you came in looking for?" The calmness starts to crack at the realization when I turn the pliers in my palms. Holding them tightly, I backhand him. The surprise on his face brings a smirk to Rosie's when I glance back. I guess he really thinks he will get out of this alive if he caves. Too bad I am dead set on making him just that: dead.

"Speak up when I ask you something."

Shaking himself, he speaks in a slight, meek tone. "Yeah, the... the... they sell them. The women."

"Are you telling me you gave her over to traffickers?" I growl.

I have felt everything fear offers for over a week, but the only emotion I can currently focus on is pure rage. This particular brand of wrath is a silent and deadly steel blade, not an explosive firearm.

Anger is a great motivator when put to proper use. Anger is an agent of change, and the only change I am looking forward to is the end of this man's life.

I grab his throat and force his head back.

"Tell me everything."

Hope drains from his body upon realizing his death is a guarantee, and the foolish notion that he will leave here alive is destroyed.

After that, he is less cooperative, but it only makes the rest of the game much more fun.

Evidently, torturing a man for information is cathartic. Some of the tension I bottled up begins to dissipate with each piece I take from him.

I had never understood when people say getting information out of someone is like pulling teeth. But as I take the pliers to his teeth and extract them one by one, I begin to understand. The satisfaction of literally pulling information from this man is worth the extra effort of the grueling task.

One by one, I remove his teeth, and blood begins to pool in his mouth. The barn becomes heavy with the scent of iron as his mouth turns into a fountain of blood. It pools in his mouth, causing him to gag and desperately gasp for air. But each attempt is futile, and the gurgling sound satisfies a sick part of me that wants this man to choke on his own blood. I want him to suffocate in it until he dies.

I am far too focused on the sight before me to notice anything beyond the man's gasping breath and terrified eyes.

For extra measure, I go over to the tools table and pick up a small knife. Its weight in my hand is a heady feeling. Part of me wonders how much damage I'm capable of. It's screaming at me to find out. Another is satisfied with merely knowing.

Tears continue to stream down his face, but when he sees the knife I hold, all of the pain painting his features is immediately replaced by panic.

I grasp him by the chin and force his mouth open for the final time.

He has a few teeth left, but I'm not concerned anymore. We have what we need from him. All that is left is his death.

Taking the pliers in my right hand, I catch hold of his tongue and pull it taught, and with the knife in my left, I begin to carve.

All of the red dripping out of his mouth and onto the floor is mesmerizing. It's a beautiful and horrid image to witness. But all I can think of as I look on is how the color would look on Julia.

I want to see her painted in it. She will be a warrior in their blood. An unstoppable force fueled by their suffering.

Coming out of the trancelike state I slipped into, I look back at Rosie. She seems satisfied and gives me a nod. I know we got what we wanted from him.

Most of all, his end.

ONE MORE HABIT

Griffin

I'm so eager to get back to Juliana I probably run more red lights than any member of HPD should. But being so far from her for even the smallest amount of time is suffocating.

How can a person become attached so quickly?

I keep questioning where these strong emotions come from but can't find a source.

It's her.

Her essence draws me in. I want to bask in the light she brings. I've barely spoken a handful of words to her and received even less, but they're all precious. She feels valuable to me.

I can only hope Quinn understands how much this matters. How important this is. Thankfully the other detective seems to somewhat understand. And the friend she mentioned—at least there's someone else out there who feels the same kind of protectiveness towards Jules. The thought of another person being so deeply invested in her life doesn't bother me. I'd rather know she has people around her who love and support her than live with the idea she's alone.

Right now, that's exactly where she is. Alone in the Mathieson Enterprises compound. Threats are everywhere, and she isn't truly safe. I've only been gone for a mere three hours, but who knows what could happen in that time. Someone could come looking for me and discover her. Is she strong enough to get out of bed? To defend herself? Would she have time to hide?

What if she left?

A shiver goes down my spine at the thought.

No. That would be a good thing. Unlikely as it is.

There's no way for her to get out without help. There's security that I run and watchful eyes in the building. That's the whole point of reaching out to Quinn. I need help if I'm going to get her to safety. It's all that really matters.

My thoughts wander on the drive.

Nice as it would be to fantasize about a future with Jules and how blissful we could be, the reality is much murkier. But it's the reality I have to deal with. I can figure out the rest later.

If she... No, *when* she gets out, she may leave, but I'll seek her out. I can't pretend we never met. That there isn't a magnetic pull between us. She's my center of gravity, and I'll forever be drawn to her. Now that we've met, I don't think I'll ever be able to leave her.

I arrive back at the compound in time for shift change, which is best suited for avoiding people in the hallways, though the security cameras are still an issue. I hope Arrick won't be checking them for anything suspicious.

There's no reason to leave the compound since I've only just returned, and I don't want to navigate whatever questions he'd ask if he knew. Nothing seems to get past the bastard.

I hate him.

The rot of his soul leaves stains on everything he touches. He has a Midas touch, but his effect is more destructive than creating gold. He causes decay everywhere he goes.

Finally, I arrive back at my door. Nothing looks unusual. No scratches or dents on the door. No splinters around the frame. Everything looks as it did when I left.

Placing my key in the door, I hold my breath until I hear the lock disengage. I open the door slowly to avoid disturbing or spooking Jules. She's lying on her side, breathing evenly. It appears she's sleeping.

I close the door behind me and fasten every lock and deadbolt before making my way over to her side. I hesitate at first, but then decide it's alright to sit beside her sleeping form at the edge of the bed.

Some hair has fallen in her face, and I reach out to

brush it away. When my fingers graze her face, I feel her tense, and I freeze. She turns her head and looks at me with her sleep-filled eyes. They are a beautiful silver-blue with flecks of almost purple in them, like geodes cracked in half.

The tension in her body flees when she finally processes who I am. I catch what looks like the beginning of a smile on her lips and can't help but grin back at her.

"Hey there."

"You're back."

Internal shivers roll through me at the sound of her melodic voice. It's good to hear, and you can tell her strength is returning by the solid tone finding its way back.

"How are you?"

My hand is near her face, and I can't help but drag my fingers down her neck as I retreat. When she reaches for me, I worry my touch is unwanted. But as she tightens her grip on my hand and pulls, I relax.

"Come 'ere." She tugs me forward.

"You want me to..." I search for the appropriate word. "Lie with you?"

The small noise of affirmation she lets out makes my heart soar. This is not the behavior I would expect from a woman who has survived a man like Arrick. The fact she wants my touch is the greatest gift I can be given. I want to hold her, touch her, kiss her, but I would never want to do anything without her permission.

So much was already taken from her. I won't add to that.

Toeing off my shoes, I move to lie beside her. My hand remains firmly in her grasp, and my arm drapes across her waist. She wriggles back a bit when I settle in and embrace her fully. Some part of this woman trusts me, and I cling to the warmth the thought brings. I bring myself up onto my elbow so I can see her face.

"I have to tell you something," I murmur.

"Later."

"Okay." I feel her drift off, and I lie there studying her while she sleeps. I will never get over how beautiful she is.

Leaning in to smell her deeply, my nose brushes her neck, and her face turns towards me. Without a thought, I journey up her neck and place a delicate kiss at the soft corner of her jaw. The hum she emits brings levity to my tired soul.

We lie there like that for a while, and I watch over her to make sure there are no disturbances. I sense her becoming restless as some dream seems to take over. Her skin turns hot, and her whole body begins to shake. Something's wrong; she's lost in a dream. I can see the anxiety manifest on her face.

I want to help her. I want to bring her out from

wherever she's lost herself. It pains me to see her like this.

I remember that my abuela used to sing to me when I was young whenever I was frightened. The same tune every time, though I don't know the lyrics. I start to hum in hopes it will soothe her.

The rough melody seems to calm her, and as she calms down, the nightmare overtaking her slumbering thoughts dissipates. It hurts to see her in distress. It isn't something I want to repeat.

It all happens in a flash, but I wonder if this is how it is and will be for her every night. That she will suffer through nightmares that make her whole body seize with fear. That she'll be dragged back into those memories by herself every night she's alone.

I lay there watching her until she wakes up and turns to face me.

"We really do need to talk," I say. My fingers run through her hair.

She nods, giving me permission to continue.

"Are you hungry? Thirsty?" I shouldn't, but it's all I can do to delay telling her everything. She deserves to know, but I don't want to get her hopes up. What if I fail her? What if I'm unable to protect her in the end?

She shakes her head, staring at me curiously. "Something's wrong."

The words are flat coming from her lips. Devoid

of all emotion, the phrase is evidence of a protective shield going up.

I hate it.

I hate seeing her defenses go up around me. I don't want to be that kind of a person to her.

"Yeah. No. Well." I'm not a man who's great with words, but it seems especially true around her. It's as though everything becomes clearer around her, but at the same time, everything is more confusing. And I'm constantly falling all over myself around her.

"I left earlier." She nods. "I went to visit with some-one."

I have no idea how to tell her. I don't really have any more details than when I left Quinn earlier. Yes, I know people are looking for her, but there's no way to be sure of what I'm sending her back to.

Even if I can get her out of here safely, I have no idea what her life on the outside is like. The threats within the compound are known, and I can do my best to protect her. But the second she's gone, that security is gone. She could be well taken care of, but what if I send her back to something as bad as this or worse?

"Look, I don't really know where to start," I say.

She looks up at me with such trust, and I don't want to sacrifice that for anything. "The beginning, maybe?" It almost seems like she's trying to joke with me. Almost.

"I told you my name is Griffin, Griffin Reyes. Everyone here knows me as Perez though."

She looks at me quizzically.

It feels so good to tell someone. It's been years since I've been one hundred percent myself. I've been living as Griffin Perez for the past four years, not Griffin Reyes. Granted, I got to keep my given name purely because I'm shit at responding to anything else. But I like the relief that comes with unfolding the truth for this woman.

"I'm a cop, and I've been here a while trying to help the department build a case against Arrick Mathieson. The guy whose office you were in." I pause, hoping for a reaction. Some kind of indication of how she's feeling as I reveal everything to her, but she gives none.

"I left today to go talk with my handler. Another cop I keep in touch with. He's a decent guy. A friend." This clearly gets her attention. "People are looking for you, Jules. Someone reported you missing, and a detective is working on your case. Evidently, the friend who reported you missing is very pushy."

"Jay." She sighs, and it seems like she's happy about it.

I momentarily tense at her reaction to the mention of another man who has such a strong reaction to her disappearance. The larger part of me is grateful to him. He will keep her safe if I can't.

"Yeah, well evidently, he's been making a lot of noise and won't go away. So the detective and my handler are going to talk with the lieutenant about putting together an operation to move both cases forward."

The look on her face is riddled with questions.

"We're working on getting you out of here."

She bolts upright with a groan and turns to me fully. She sways a little, so I sit up and put my hands on her shoulders to steady her.

When she's steady, she speaks. "You want to let me leave?"

"Of course."

"I thought..." She pauses, and I wait for her to finish. "I thought I was supposed to stay? I thought you were supposed to keep me. I thought you were going to keep me."

I didn't realize that's how she sees me, as her captor. Or maybe her protector. It squeezes at my heart that she thinks I would force her to stay. That I would force her to do anything.

"No, I need you away from here. I need you away from Arrick. I asked my friend to work on a plan to get you out."

She sits frozen for a moment, and then her hands move to cup my face. She studies me for a moment, and I feel the warmth of her soft lips press to mine.

XII

GODDESS

Juliana

'm kissing him, and I want it. I like it more than I care to admit.

I just met this man, yet I know he's trustworthy. I know he's safe.

Now I'm kissing him?

Logically it makes no sense, but it feels right.

My hands stay holding his face, and I expect him to reach for me. For him to touch me in some way. I expect him to grab me by the hips or thrust his hands into my hair. To take over.

Instead, I feel him melt. He sinks into the kiss and into me.

And it feels good. Our lips are pressed together, and it feels like we're seeking the other within the kiss. After a moment of impatience, I bite slightly at his lip and hear a sharp intake of breath. He opens for me, and I take what's mine. I explore him until we're both breathless and panting. Then I pull away slightly.

I can feel him follow, and his forehead comes to rest against my own. It's evident he misses my touch, but he never reaches for me or pushes for more. Not going to lie, the small high I feel from his restraint is thrilling.

Glancing down, I can see the evidence of his arousal, and I feel powerful knowing I've put him in this state. That I have that kind of effect on him.

Internally, I'm warring with myself. I shouldn't want him. Especially not like this.

It's reckless and impulsive.

But my heart and my body have different ideas. They're winning too.

His eyes are still closed, and he's waiting for me. He needs me to make the next move and decide where this is heading. I have a feeling if I wanted it to, everything would stop without a moment's hesitation.

When my hand leaves his face, he opens his eyes. Staring straight into mine, he looks at me with such reverence.

He will never hurt me.

Not like that man.

He will never put his hands on me and force me to my knees. Never bind me so I'm helpless when thrown on a table, my knees pushed apart.

A small touch on my thigh brings me back to the moment, and the worry in Griffin's eyes makes my pussy throb.

With my free hand, I turn and lightly push him back onto the bed. He falls with no hesitancy and puts his hands above his head. And all of his free will.

No one has ever given up control to me before. I never thought I would want someone to, but the weight of his trust settles over me. I feel the need for control building, and he's giving it to me. I feel drunk with power. The quick flip between despair and raging lust sends me reeling. I want to shove my darker thoughts down and live in the fiery lust building between us.

I want to be reckless with this man. Or rather, I want this man to be reckless with me.

"What do you want?" I ask.

I need him to say it out loud. I want him to confess he needs me to take over as much as I want to.

"What you need," he says, his voice breathy. The simple truth of the statement sends a thrilling shiver through me.

"I need control. I need to be in charge." His little nods of approval encourage me to continue. "I need your hands to stay above your head. No touching. Can you do that?" His final nod gives me the permission I need.

I let my hands drift to his chest, and my fingers explore all of the rippling muscles beneath his shirt. They journey to his arms and over the tattoos that only earlier today I craved to touch.

"How many do you have?" I ask.

"Would you like to see them all?"

Slowly he rises and reaches for the hem of his T-shirt. Drawing up the fabric is the unveiling of a masterwork in a museum. Every inch of his body is covered in tattoos. All of them bursting with color and life.

"Yeah, I saw some of them earlier. They're beautiful. I wanted to explore them. To know what they were. You were on your knees then by the bed. I liked you there."

"On my knees?"

"Yes," I say. It could be odd to ask this of him, but the way he's looking at me says he needs me to instruct and guide. Both for his benefit and mine.

It seems he understands immediately as he takes my hands and guides me to the edge of the bed. With my legs hung over the side, he slides off to kneel in front of me.

"Do you like having me on my knees?" I can only squeeze his hand in reply.

He looks so beautiful there, looking up at me. The reverence on his face is apparent, and I feel so seen. His undivided attention is intoxicating, and I want to drown in the sensation. For days my nerves have been on fire, every part of me on high alert. But in his presence, looking at him from above, those fears and anxieties start to dwindle. The boiling rage and gripping fear are edged out by a better, more peaceful state of mind.

Sleep has been elusive as of late, and I know part of me is searching for a moment of peace. I should be concerned I'm seeking out that feeling with someone I just met. Still, my heart feels no hesitation about trusting Griffin with my vulnerabilities. All of them.

Grounding myself around him is easier than when alone. It doesn't matter how many cracks in the ceiling I count or how many times I recite lists in my head to try and calm my frantically racing heart—peace is a struggle to find. Still, the vision of Griffin kneeling in front of me with all of his vivid tattoos and sculpted muscles on display gives me a presence of mind that's been missing since I was first dragged into that other room.

I study him for a while, letting my eyes journey up and down his body while he waits patiently. I move at my own pace. Never does he push me. He never demands anything. He remains motionless and follows the expressions on my face as I explore him.

I turn his hand to reveal the delicate skin at his wrist. I want to know the story of every line on his body. I want the history of every scar, scratch, and ink mark composing his life's story.

Starting there at his wrist, I touch along the patterns that are permanently etched into his skin and silently implore him to tell the story of each one.

"The lilies are each for a friend I've lost," he says. I continue the journey up his arm, and he lets out a laugh when I reach the tattoo on his shoulder. "It's from a friend when he was first getting into tattooing. He gave me my first stick and poke when we were in middle school." He shows me his opposite wrist where a crooked smiley face lies. "He started as an apprentice about the same time I was applying to the academy. He bet me if I got in on my first try, he would give me my first real tat to fit in better. It's when I got addicted."

We continue like this for a while. My hands trail over his body as he maps out his life. The heat building between us is undeniable, but I don't want to break the trance we're in. It's so good, and I don't want to ruin it.

When I reach the space above his heart, I'm struck by the empty space alongside two other names.

"My abuela and my sister. Abuela passed a year after I graduated high school."

"And your sister?"

He sighed. "She got sick—leukemia—and we couldn't afford to get her the treatment she needed. She passed when I was nine; she was six."

There's no response to that kind of history. I can only sit there until he speaks.

"I wanted to keep space there so I could have the names of the most important people in my life right by my heart."

I run my fingers back and forth across the small blank space, pondering what he could possibly mean when he takes hold of my hand. The pure adoration in his eyes, and quite possibly love, make me think it's for me, but that couldn't possibly be true. We don't know each other. We just met.

"What do you need, Jules?"

His nickname for me sends shivers up my spine. But dread fills my chest at the question. I hate that question. I hate being asked what I want and need. I don't like feeling like a burden, so I don't spend much time thinking about myself. It's easier to focus on everyone else.

I shake my head, trying to get him to change the subject. He doesn't give up.

"Please, precious, tell me what I can do."

His pleading makes me crumble. My need for control is new—normally I don't like making decisions—but the last straw is seeing him look up at me, begging.

I can feel a sob clutching at my chest, but I don't want to break down. Not now. Not when everything's so simple. Not when everything else that's happened is momentarily less painful. I don't want to ruin it with the overwhelming feelings lurking beneath the surface. So I trap them in the recesses of my mind and push them back until all I can feel is the warmth of his hands engulfing mine and the need building in my core.

The war between my head and body is raging at full force. Some part of me needs him desperately. Needs him to kiss me, touch me, fuck me. Another part of me is wary of that kind of intimacy. The twisting in my stomach at the idea of him hovering over me makes me nauseous and weak. I'm so conflicted it feels like there is no decision to make. All of them are the wrong ones.

"Touch me." My body wins out over my head. "I want your hands on me. I need to feel something good."

The desperation in my words is embarrassing, but he looks at me with understanding.

Moving slowly, he grasps me by the hips and pulls me farther toward the edge of the bed. My legs fall open to him, and he fits himself between them. He belongs there. His hands begin to drag down my thighs over the sweatpants he dressed me in, and I relax into the caress. It's so careful and tender. He moves slowly enough not to startle me, and every movement and touch brings my walls down a little further.

Fingers skim across my inner thighs tentatively, the feeling soaking through the soft fabric, and my sighs of appreciation seem to encourage him. He works his way up until his touch is barely shy of where I need him. Seeing my content expression, he stops there and lingers. Then he frustratingly moves away and starts to run his palms along my sides and ribs. He carefully avoids the wounds hidden under the bandages he so carefully wrapped me in, but there are small unavoidable flashes of pain that only serve to heighten the pleasure his touch brings me.

When he reaches my breasts, I nearly lose all thought. Bra lost to the carnage of my captor, he cups and fondles them. Studies them through the thin white shirt I'm wearing over my bandaged body. Impatience seems to take over him for a moment, and he reaches to pull up my shirt.

My hand shoots out to stop the movement.

"No," I command.

Understanding dawns on him, and he backs down. He took care of me when I was at my worst. He knows what bruises are healing and which cuts will scar. He knows the reminder that those things are for me, and I admire that he doesn't push me to fulfill his own desires.

He lowers the hem of my shirt back down, but only moments later, I feel his hands rise beneath the fabric. The warmth of his hands on me is soothing, and I relax as he explores the feel of my bandaged body. I suck in a breath when he grazes his thumbs across my nipples, and an intense need lights in me. His thumbs flutter back and forth over the taught nubs, and my desire flames further as he circles the sensitive skin.

He continues to caress and work my breasts, but

he never rises up to kiss me. Impatience taking over, I firmly grasp his hands where they cup me, and I lean down to kiss him. When our lips connect, he rises up farther onto his knees, seeking more from me. I guide him in the kiss, sucking and biting at him. Our tongues intertwine in each other as we drive ourselves closer.

The bed is low to the ground and, finally, we're close enough that my cunt is lightly pressed to his cock. I feel him continue to press into me, and my heated core grinds into him through the fabric of our clothes. When I start to fall back with him above me, fear shoots through me, and my hand reaches out desperately to grab him by the throat.

He stops, but there's a renewed fire in his eyes. He likes this. My hand forcefully grabbing his neck turns him on.

A name crosses my mind, and I wonder what his reaction will be.

"Stay on the ground where you belong, pet."

In another life, this man would wear my collar.

The endearment makes him grin, and I know my feeling was correct. This man wants—no, craves—my control. He wants to submit to me in whatever way I desire. The rush the thought brings me is thrilling.

I decide to embrace the fantasy.

"You like this, don't you? Do you like when I choke you?" I tighten my hand around his throat. "Do you like it when I call you pet?"

He manages to get out a breathy yes through my grip.

"Do you want to be a good boy for me?" I push him back down on his knees and lean over him. My hand loosens its grip so he can respond.

"Yes. Whatever you want. I'll do whatever you want."

Emboldened by his compliance, I let go of him. My fingers move to take his chin and tilt his face up towards me.

"Are you hungry, pet?" I phrase it as a question, but it's a statement. "Do you deserve to taste me?"

"Please." I've never witnessed someone plead, but it feels good to hear his desperation and hunger. I realize I like it, too. The puzzle pieces of our desire lock together—his need for my control, and my need to take it.

I lift my hips off the bed slightly. "Take them off."

Slowly, his hands rise to the edge of the sweatpants, and he begins to draw them down. When they reach my ankles, I speak.

"Take them off. I want to see you kiss and nip and bite your way up to my pussy."

His face snaps to look at me, but it's not out of confusion. It's lust.

He does as asked, and the feel of his lips, his teeth, and his tongue on my skin fans my desire hotter and higher. There's a gentleness to his touch, and my head tips back; I sink into the feeling and the thrill skimming across my body.

When the sensation stops, I look back down at him to find him looking at me with a whisper of a smile on his lips. Simply looking. Being the center of a person's attention, admired so closely, is a heady feeling. The intimate weight of the moment presses against a part of my heart that's been neglected. I feel seen. Truly seen by him.

Overwhelmed, I grab him by the hair and pull him where I want him—my cunt. At the closeness, my knees fall farther apart, and I sigh in pleasure.

"May I taste you? Please?" he asks.

His words send two kinds of warmth spreading through my body. One directed at my heart and the other at my cunt, which is pulsing desperately.

"You may, pet."

Immediately, he is on me. His movements are desperate, and damn is he good with his mouth. One strong lick sends shivers up my spine, but it's the smaller drags of the flat of his tongue that have me building towards my release. He's so attentive to my reactions, repeating circular motions that make my hips kick up or increasing the rhythm of the tip of his tongue as it flicks at my clit.

"Yes. Yes, that," I pant.

The encouragement lights something in him, and his hands move towards my pussy.

"More. I want your fingers in me."

Without hesitation, he takes a finger and thrusts it into me. My back arches at the intrusion, and my arms start to shake while trying to keep me upright. Before I can fully adjust to the feeling, he adds a second, and my head falls back as I groan.

His movements are slow and fluid, which conflict with the actions of his mouth. His free hand trails over my body, exploring every inch as he focuses on my pleasure. I fall fully back on the bed as the dual sensations press me closer and closer to the edge. When he increases the pressure of his strokes against the most sensitive spot, I think I might die. But it's nothing compared to when he crosses those two fingers and rocks them against me.

The sensation overwhelms, and I fall over the edge, deep into my pleasure.

Then he shocks me by guiding me back from the pleasurable abyss I escape to. He continues to stroke and suck and lick until I return to the present with him. My body slowly recovers from my shaken ecstasy.

When I realize I had fallen back onto the bed, I lift my head to look down at him. He's grinning from ear to ear, and when our eyes meet, he bends to give me a final kiss on the sensitive skin of my inner thigh.

I groan at the sight.

"You really enjoyed yourself, didn't you?" I ask the question softly, hoping he doesn't hear it.

"Of course."

Everything with Griffin is complex and simple. The constant push and pull of opposing forces create a dangerous dynamic between us. I want more time with him.

I am grateful he's here and wants to help me. A part of me needs to get as far away from this place as I possibly can, but another part of me feels a pull towards this man, telling me I need to keep him close.

"So, what now?" I ask.

"Now you sleep." He stands as he speaks. "And I wait to hear from my friend."

It seems like a simple enough plan.

When he turns away, I clasp his arm firmly. "Don't leave. Not yet. Not again."

He turns back to me with a heartbreaking look in his eyes. It's a look speaking of unending loyalty and sacrifice, but there's hurt mixed in. As if he knows his fate. Our fate.

"I won't leave you unless I have to, okay?" he says as he crawls into bed with me, pulling the covers around us.

I don't like his response, but I see the truth in his words. He wouldn't leave. Not without me, it seems.

Not without doing everything he can to protect me.

He won't leave.

Not unless he has to.

XIII

LOVE LIKE MINE

Juliana

Waking up next to Griffin is a new kind of peace. In the middle of a living nightmare, I've found tranquility, and I cling to him.

Snuggling closer, I sense when he wakes up. In our slumber, I've wrapped myself around him like a snake does its prey, but unlike the snake, my prey is holding on to me equally tightly. It seems Griffin, too, is incapable of letting me go too far from him.

"Hey, how'd you sleep?" he asks.

Hearing the question out loud, I realize I slept through the night. There were no nightmares. No terrors to fight in my sleep.

"Better."

"Good." He kisses my forehead.

I love small moments of affection like that. We lie there for a moment, enjoying the peaceful quiet.

"I need to get an update from Quinn. I'll have to leave, okay?" I nod, understanding, but I still don't want him to go. It seems neither does he. His arms are wrapped around me, and his hand absentmindedly brushes through my hair.

"I'll make you something to eat." He struggles to pull away.

The offer makes me smile. Last night I discovered a new quality to this man, and I realize this is part of who he is. He's a caretaker and protector, similar to how I am with so many of the people I love. The difference is my selflessness tends to be a part of my search for love and approval. I like to feel needed, and it's draining sometimes. It's the opposite for Griffin; it's like his need to do things for me brings him fulfillment. There seems to be a purpose to him I don't quite understand.

It's sweet. He's sweet. It's all so sickeningly sweet.

Finally, we unwrap ourselves from each other. Griffin pulls out a shirt and pants to wear and heads into the kitchen.

The tranquil moment is broken by a ringing fire alarm going off, and loud thundering noises begin in the hall.

Griffin looks back at me, panicked and unsure. He springs into action and starts shoving items at me as he speaks. "You need to get dressed. I don't know what's happening. Quinn should have called me or given me warning if they were doing anything, but even if this isn't them, we need to use this to get you out, okay?"

I see the moment where his thoughts switch over. He's in full protector mode. The gears are turning, and the man is making plans.

I'm still wearing his shirt, but rush to put on the discarded pair of pants from last night and the boots in front of me. My body screams with every movement, but I understand the stakes. Probably more than he does. I'd been in that room for days. He hadn't. If anyone knows how desperately people need to stay away from this place, it's me.

Only I want to stay.

With Griffin.

The appearance of guns shouldn't startle me, but it's the first moment when reality sets in. This is real. I have an opportunity to escape the man who took me, kept me, *hurt* me. I can go back to Jay and my friends and my life.

But what about Griffin?

As he crosses my path once more, I reach out to grab him by the collar of the jacket he threw on and stop him in front of me. "Griffin, what happens after?"

"What do you mean, what happens after? You're out, and we get you somewhere safe."

"And you do what? Go back to this? Alone?"

It finally seems to dawn on him what I'm asking about.

Us. What happens to *us* after. That's the real question.

This shouldn't be our immediate concern. Things need to happen, and everything will move quickly. But this moment feels vital. After what we've shared over the past week and what happened last night, I can't walk away. I need him whether he wants to be there for me or not. I hope he does, but ultimately, I can't leave him.

"Look, right now, we focus on getting you back to your boyfriend, okay?" His expression goes blank at the term. "I can promise you this, I will never walk away from you. Not for anything. Not ever."

The conviction in his tone calms the anxiousness that constricts my throat. Even after a short time, I have attached a part of myself to this man. He's mine, and I won't go without him.

There's a loud bang on the door.

"Griffin, open up." The voice calls over the sounding alarms.

The man in question turns to me. "Hide."

I grab the things around me and rush to the bathroom. Once I shut myself in, I hear Griffin open the door. I'm barely able to hear their muffled conversation.

Griffin speaks first in a harsh tone he's never used with me. "Report."

"Someone got into the warehouse and set off a fire in

the lab. Most of it won't be salvageable from the looks of it. They've disabled the security system, sprinklers, and ventilation systems. Several techs are injured or dead from the fumes already. I was in the security office, and we saw a glimpse of two intruders before everything went dark. We don't have eyes anymore. Boss is paranoid and went into lockdown in his office."

With no hesitation or change in his tone, Griffin responds. "Okay, radio everyone. I want a full sweep of the building. Starting at the top. I'll start with this corridor and work my way down."

"Start at the top? Shouldn't we—"

The man didn't get to finish the thought. "I said top. Your job isn't to think. Only do."

"Yes, sir."

I hear the man begin talking on what I can only assume is their radio system before he gets cut off by the sound of Griffin closing the door.

Footsteps quickly approach the bathroom, and I tense even though I know who it is. Griffin opens the door, and I relax as he steps towards me.

"Good, you're dressed. We need to move quickly. Have you ever used a gun before?"

I roll my eyes at him. "This is Texas. Of course I've used a gun. Only for hunting though."

The corner of his mouth jerks up in a small smirk. His eyes sparkle with pride.

"Let's get you gone then." The confidence in his voice reassures me, but I can't help but hear the tinge of sadness accompanying the words.

Guns in hand, we make it down the hallway towards the stairs. I wait out of sight at each turn until Griffin confirms no one's coming. His body is coiled tightly, and there's a singular focus in his movements.

Making our way into the first-floor hallway, we spot two bodies lying on the ground as we round the corner. Though we don't really have the time, Griffin pauses to check on one of the men. He almost looks like he's sleeping, but Griffin hangs his head after searching for a pulse. The other has a deep gash across his throat, and blood is pooling around his head. You can see the staining on his lips where the blood disrupted whatever desperate attempts the man made at breathing in the end.

Without warning, a hand covers my mouth, and I'm locked into the grasp of an unknown stranger. I let out a muffled scream. Griffin turns back to me with a feral look on his face.

Confused, I try to turn to see my attacker, who does nothing more than keep me in place, but I can feel their tall, lithe body pressed up against my own. I can't turn enough to see who holds me, but the slight pivot of my head reveals a black man who's only an arm's length away from Griffin. I try to warn him, but Griffin's attention is fixated on me.

The stranger reaches out, and I see the glint of a knife in his hand, but before he can get close enough, Griffin catches sight of him.

Griffin grabs the outwardly stretched hand of the attacker and twists it behind his back. With a swift kick to the back of his knees, the man falls to the floor and Griffin has them pinned. The man looks murderous.

I want to lick the beads of sweat off Griffin's body. All of his muscles are taught with rage as he speaks. "Let Jules go, or I end your partner."

I can only assume the figure who holds me is in shock by the way their body tenses.

"Wait, we're only here for her. Juliana." The speaker releases me, and I turn to face them. My calm returns with Griffin at my back. "Jay Maddox sent us."

Jay?

I'm shocked. Since when is Jay involved with these types of people? People who set buildings on fire and, by the dark stains on their black clothing, kills people. I grab at the back of Griffin's jacket, and he looks back at me tentatively. The moment is tense, but I have to trust my instincts.

"If Jay sent them, then we have to trust them."

"Jules, I'm not trusting you with strangers just because they supposedly know your friend."

"I'm Cy. That's Ember." The guy in Griffin's hold grunts out. "No longer strangers."

He searches my face for any sign of hesitation, but I don't give anything to him. I have to trust Jay knows what he's doing.

"Griffin, there's no time. I trust Jay. Trust me, please."

Slowly Griffin releases his grip on the man he has pinned to the floor. As he rises, I notice the tattoos that run up his left arm. When I reach his face, I feel caught by his gaze.

"I'm hoping you have a plan to get her out of here?" He says.

The stranger who held me speaks. "Well, that got shot to hell when we heard them radio, they were starting their sweep at the top of the building. We planned for a rooftop exit."

"Yeah, that was me. I wanted time to get her down without any interruptions. I'm guessing the fire and security system was you two?"

The man rising from the floor grunts in affirmation.

I look at the two strangers before me, each clearly built for combat, but one more solidly than the other. The man, Cy, stands several inches taller than me and the other, Ember, is his equal in height. They're a balanced pair, and each seems to anticipate the movements of the other as if by second nature.

Griffin studies the pair, just as I had, trying to decide if they're trustworthy. I know we can, though. How else would they know to tell me Jay's involved?

Still holding on to his jacket, I give it a tug to bring Griffin's attention back to me. He must see my plea because he backs away from the man next to him, angling his body in front of my own.

"Let's get you out of here then." His words are soft, and I know there is a little bit of sadness mixed in too.

I know how he feels. Everything is happening so quickly. I'm not ready to let him go either.

Griffin takes the lead and heads back the way our new companions came. His pace increases and despite my long legs, I have to almost jog to keep up.

I hate running.

At every corner, door, and intersection, Griffin or one of the others go about checking to make sure no one's in our way. When there is... one of them rounds the corner, and then there is no one. I never see them, and I know Griffin at least is doing it to shield me from this bit of violence.

The last door we go through opens up into a garage, with large open bay doors leading to a street outside.

Then everything settles in my mind, and I fully process what's happening. I'm leaving with complete strangers, trusting they were telling the truth about Jay.

My feet stick in place.

I watch as Griffin grabs keys off the wall and exchanges it with one of the others. I see them take a set of keys and unlock a car. A very nice car. But I can't bring myself to move.

Even if this is over and I'm heading home, I know things won't be the same, which scares me more than I care to admit. I know returning to my life won't feel normal. Something in me says I'll never have that again. That kind of ignorance. This will stay with me and color every moment of my future.

I'm not prepared for it.

From this moment forward, my life will be various degrees of suffering.

Before Griffin, I was trapped in a place between life and death. Not purgatory per se, but a place entirely void of everything. There, a man took hold of me and crushed down on my soul to a point where life became a meaningless word, and hope was forgotten entirely. The moments of respite I found with Griffin are real, but they're a distraction. Once he walks away, and he will walk away, I'll be back to the haunting emptiness.

My body has turned to ice, and I only notice Griffin is standing before me when the warmth of his hands settles onto my shoulders. I step closer to him, hoping to retain some of the feeling. Some of him.

"You have to leave now," he whispers.

His interruption of the deafening silence in my ears forces out the thought circulating my mind. "You're going back, aren't you?"

"I have to. I have a job to do here. I can't disappear."

"But you can with me."

"No, never. Not forever."

"You'll find me?" I hate the tremor in my voice.

"Every time."

His lips touch softly to mine, and we disappear into one another. The rumble of the car starting brings us out of the trance we fell into. I feel his lips press against the center of my forehead, and I soak up his last touch. I cling to him while breathing in his lemon and clove scent. I try to memorize everything about him before turning to walk to the car.

The pair is standing outside of the car doors, and they climb in when they see me approaching. I feel Griffin following me and his warmth wraps around me as he reaches to open the car door. I don't want to step away from him, not now. I turn back to him slightly and he kisses my temple before I force myself to get into the car.

Once settled, I make a mistake. I shouldn't turn to him but I do. I look back to get one more glimpse of Griffin before he closes the door and we drive off.

My fears from earlier start to consume me. The realization of how truly broken I am is overwhelming. My new scars aren't skin deep.

I can't help but think about how everyone will know. Or how they will learn about it eventually. How they'll see how damaged I am.

I wish I would have told Griffin that instead. That I'm broken and I'm not worth his affection. I wish I told him to stay away instead of asking him to come and find me. I want to hold on to the good feelings from our short time together.

If he ever finds me? All of that goodness will disappear behind the haze of obscurity now haunting me.

XIV

MOVE LIKE U STOLE IT

Ember

Cy was like a kid on Christmas when that guy, Griffin, handed him the keys to this Aston Martin. There's a particular high any time we finish an assignment, but he's especially enjoying this specific perk.

Who knew Sage's ex was such a car guy? It makes sense though by the description she gave us of the asshole. Seems he likes money, no matter how ill-gotten. He likes to spend it and show it off too.

It's kind of kismet we helped Sage and her son only a month ago and now are hired to come and rescue another woman from the same man. The dude seriously has some issues if people are fleeing him like this.

Glancing back into the back seat, I quietly observe the girl... Juliana.

She seemed so alive when she was around that guy, but it's like she shut down since we took off. Based on what I know about Arrick and the Mathieson Enterprises operations, I'm sure she's gone through hell. Her friend's concerns are definitely justified, but he'd described her so differently from how she appears.

I understand hardship and loss. Pain and violence are no strangers either in this life. It's how I met Cy. How we came together. It was love at first gunshot.

This girl seems lost in a different kind of way than I've ever experienced. Only time will tell how she'll come out of this.

Looking at her, there's a certain quality I can't quite name. It's like when you buy a candle but never light it. There's a purpose, but its value is placed on its existence and potential rather than the fulfillment of potential.

I'd be curious to see what this woman looks like as her most authentic self. I'd bet she's a force to be reckoned with.

As we drive, I can't help but continue to glance back at her. Every time I do, she's sunken deeper into herself. She's closing herself off from everything in anticipation of some sort of malicious yet unknown force.

Every glance has an odd concern growing in my chest for this woman. It's not something I normally experience with people. Cy is one of the few people in this world I've any real attachment to. We've been together for thirteen years, and I know him almost as well as I know myself.

This unfamiliar feeling is kind of unsettling but only a little unwanted.

Pulling into the garage space at the firehouse we've made our home base, I look back at her. At some point, she fell asleep, exhausted from recent events.

"Cy, we should probably call Sage. She's a doctor?"

"Why? We were hired to get her and get her back to the friend in one piece," Cy grumbles.

Idiot clearly hasn't caught up yet. I love him, but sometimes he's slower than molasses.

"I don't think we can do that yet. We found her once easily enough. Nothing to say they won't rinse and repeat. Plus, clearly, she went through something back there. She looks even worse than when we tracked down Sage and Kieran."

"Fine then, call Sage. Get her to help, but I'm done here."

Maybe Cy's got more feelings than he's letting on. He's not normally so gruff towards people. Especially not clients. Quiet, maybe, but not dismissive.

"Can you at least carry her in while I get everything unpacked? I'll call Sage and see when she can be here. She still in the Galleria safehouse?"

Looks like I'll only be getting nods and grunts from now on, but I take it.

Halfway to the elevator with Juliana in his arms, Cy calls back, "And call the friend. I want him out of our shit. The flower girl who started this shit too. Pair of 'em are annoying as fuck."

I huff. His mood isn't making any sense, but I don't have time to worry about that. After being together for thirteen years, you think you know everything about your partner, but sometimes they surprise you. This is one of those times where I leave him to sulk on his own for a while.

I call Sage first, wanting to put off the call to the friend. After a few rings, she picks up.

"Hey, is everything okay? Do we need to move again? Does Kieran need to stay home from camp today?"

"Nah, no need to worry. But we do need your help. We picked up a girl, and she's in bad shape."

"Oh, Lord, of course. Can you send someone to come get us like last time?"

"Yeah, I'll send Ash over." I can hear her sigh in relief. I know she's struck up a friendship of sorts with Ash, and I'm comfortable trusting her with Sage's safety. "Sage, you need to know..."

I really don't know how to tell her. I should have done this before, when we got the contract.

Knowing it hasn't been long, I can only hope the emotional wounds won't reopen. The woman has already done so much since she left Arrick. She's strong, but everyone has a breaking point.

"The girl we were hired to get? The person who hired us pointed us to Mathieson Enterprises."

A sharp intake of breath comes over the phone.

"She was with him, wasn't she?" she asks.

"Well, yes, kinda. I'll explain more when you get here, alright?"

"Yeah. Okay. I'll bring the supplies I have on hand, but if you send word with Ash about her injuries, I can put together a list for her to go and pick up."

"Got it. Be safe. And bring the kid. We miss him around here. It's been a while."

It's good to hear the small laugh she lets out. The little moments of joy are important for them.

"I'll tell him you miss him."

"Oh, don't do that. He'll get the wrong idea." The laughter in my voice is a betrayal. "He'll start to think we're buds or something."

I hang up the phone and go about unloading our bags and putting all the equipment back in the weapons room.

It's only been in the past couple of years that we finally took over and established a real landing place for all of us in our network, The Ascendancy Collective. Most of our associates come and go as needed. It's only Cy and me here full time. But it's home for us, despite the overwhelming number of guns, explosives, tactical equipment, and other items in our literal arsenal.

I cross the garage to the spiral staircase and pull my phone back out.

Calling this dude, and especially telling him what state Juliana is in, is going to be hard. Cy likes to leave me with the hard crap. Some would accuse him of not giving a shit, but the reality is he gets too emotionally involved. He struggles with detaching himself; it's better than in the past, but at some point, we fell into a pattern where I handle the people crap and he handles the technical and planning stuff.

It takes the time to rise up to the top floor before I work up the courage to call her friend from my burner. As I reach the landing, I dial. Unsurprisingly, Jay picks up on the second ring.

"Hey, I saw on the news there was some kind of upset in the port. Was that you? Did you find her?" The anxiety rolling off him through the phone is stifling.

"Dude, calm down. Let me get a few words in why don't cha?"

I know the guy is frustrated. He's been on edge since the first time his friend, Rosie, the "flower girl" as Cy likes to call her, contacted us. But seriously, he needs a sedative at this point.

"Look, we found her." I hear the breath he's holding release. "But we can't bring her back yet. Okay?"

"What do you mean?"

This dude with all of the questions. I'm so close to strangling the guy the first chance I get.

"She's not in great shape, and we're concerned they're gonna come looking for her the second they realize she's gone. Right?"

"What do you mean she's not in great shape? You think they're going to come after her? Why?"

Yup, definitely gonna strangle the dude.

"Look, your friend can probably answer some of those questions later. Right now, all you need to know is she's safe here with us, and we have a doctor coming to look at her. Lie low, and I'll be in touch when we know more," I say.

"Wait, you can't cut me out. Can I talk to her at least?"

"I know you're worried out of your mind, and I would be too, but trust me when I say the best thing you can do is sit tight."

There's silence for a second, and I hear him clear his throat as if to start on another line of questioning, but I cut him off.

"Dude. Stop. You keep pushing, and I'm hanging up on you."

Over the phone I can almost hear the gears in his mind turning. "Yeah, okay. But..." Concern leaks through. "Keep me updated? I need to know she's okay.

And tell her... tell her I miss her."

I sigh. "Yeah, I'll give you another call soon." I make my way down the hall but stop and sag on one of the walls after talking with Jay. The man's exhausting. I almost regret taking the job.

Almost.

XV

OUT OF NOWHERE

Sage

In the few short weeks we have known each other, I have learned to respond immediately when Ember or Cy calls. It's a lot like working in the ER. It's a natural rhythm for me after working in one for over a decade.

They literally saved Kieran and me. When they didn't have to. They could have fulfilled Arrick's contract and taken the money, but they didn't. I am eternally grateful. I owe them a lot, and of course I will help them anytime one of their "friends" needs help. No matter how questionable the person may be, they still need help. They're still human. Life has changed a lot, but I do still put my patients' best interests first, and it's not my place to question how or why someone gets injured.

This one is different though. It's like what they say in school: you should never take on a patient who is connected to you. The logic is that things get too personal, and you cannot remain objective in the situation.

Well, this is definitely crossing that line.

Everything to do with Arrick is personal.

Leaving him was the best decision I have ever made. He threatened our lives, but I'm still grieving. Not for the loss of the relationship, but more for the idealized man I thought him to be.

Knowing others have suffered at Arrick's hand weighs on my conscience. So Ember asking for help with the fallout feels like the least I can do. Of course I will drop everything to go and help this woman.

Not that I have much going on these days.

I start going around and picking up the various tools and supplies I need.

Working as I go, I call out to Kieran. "Hey, bud!" I yell. "I need you to pack your backpack, okay? You're not going to camp today. We are going over to see Cy and Ember."

As nine-year-old's are wont to do, Kieran runs out of his room as though his feet are on fire. He looks like a copy of me with his blonde hair, blue eyes, and round face. He's growing like a weed, and I'm grateful now for the resemblance between us. Looking at my son, he is mine, even though he has his father's nose and ears. That is one thing that Arrick cannot take from me.

"We're going to see Cy and Ember?" he asks excitedly. Then he withdraws. "Who's picking us up?"

"Ash is coming over." At my words, he lights back

up.

I understand his wariness. It is hard to adjust to a new life, and the circumstances that led to us meeting Cy and Ember makes trusting people harder than ever. The awareness of certain dangers I previously lacked was rapidly forced upon us, and, unfortunately, I am not the only one who adopted this new habit.

"Go ahead and pack for overnight, okay? I don't know how long we will be there." He starts to run off as I call after him, "And don't forget to bring your new books. Oh, and the stuff for the project you are working on with Ember. I'm sure they will want to work on it with you."

I walk around and finish pulling together my supplies, grabbing a few extra changes of clothes. I must drift off into thought at some point because I am startled back to the present by a knock on the door.

I check the camera doorbell to see who it is and sigh in relief. It's Ash.

"Hey, come in. I will go get Kieran and grab our stuff," I say.

Ash nods, and I wonder if I will ever get to have a full-blown conversation with her. At first, getting Ash to say anything at all was a struggle, and I genuinely thought she hated me, but we have built a sort of friendship. It's part of who she is, and I guess it comes with time.

I walk in to find Kieran on his bed, absorbed in his book with headphones on, backpack at his feet. He was tested when he was younger for ADHD, autism, and dyslexia because of some learning difficulties he dealt with early on. His autism diagnosis is a miracle, and once we figured out that audiobooks help him, he's been constantly reading sci-fi and mystery books. And, since meeting Ember, tinkering with whatever project they are helping him with.

As I enter, his head picks up, and he reaches to pull off the headphones.

"Ready to go, bud?"

Grabbing his bag, he turns to me with a bright smile on his face. It's so good to see him smile.

"Yup!" he exclaims, popping the *p* as he hops out of bed.

We make our way to the elevators with Ash and my nerves blossom. I don't want to ask. I don't want to know about this girl—Arrick's victim. Not yet.

As we settle into Ash's SUV, I turn back to Kieran. "Hey, bud. Why don't you put your headphones back on and read on our way over, okay?"

Before I even finish speaking, he's already digging around in his bag for his stuff.

When he is settled in, I turn to Ash. "What am I walking into, Ash?"

She sighs as if already regretting what she has to

share. "The girl is in really bad shape. Ember said some guy did his best to care for her. Based on the description they gave me though, it sounds like whatever he did was surface level." She pauses to collect herself. "Cy carried her in and started yelling for everyone to get out. Most of the Ascendancy crew is already packed up and gone."

"Oh, Lord, I guess I will see when we get there. Did Ember give you any other details? I told them I would put together a supplies list."

"Nah, none of us there know enough to be of any help, and I don't think Cy would've let us near her anyway. He's acting weird about her. He stormed through the place with the girl in his arms. I was only there for a short while before I left to come and get you."

"Okay. Thanks."

It's then that I realize we held a whole conversation. I don't think Ash has ever spoken so many words at one time. I look over in wonder before asking the question on my mind.

"Everyone's really on edge about this, aren't they? This doesn't seem normal for y'all."

"Yeah."

It was the last word spoken on the drive.

With a crumbling façade that threatens to haunt you, a normal person would feel unnerved at the sight of the old firehouse building Cy and Ember converted into their home base. It still maintains most of its original design, and Kieran loves sliding down the fireman's pole, but when you look closely, you can see the elements which have turned it into a fortress. The intimidating sight settles me though as we roll up to the garage entrance. I know we are safe in the apartment, but there is a different sense of security here.

Pulling into the garage, I can see Ember waiting for us by the stairs.

As soon as the car stops and the bay doors close, Kieran is out and running towards them, leaving me to grab his stuff as well as mine.

A mother's work and all that.

"Hey, little man," Ember teases. I can picture the massive eye roll from Kieran that accompanies the greeting.

"I'm not little," Kieran whines back.

"Yeah, yeah, yeah. You'll always be my little man though."

As I join them where they stand, Kieran tucks beneath Ember's arm. I look at them, searching for any indication of what I should be anticipating. When their face falls from the bright, cheery expression of moments ago, my dread builds.

Ember has a presence about them, likely due to their tall figure that stands several inches above my own 5' 8" frame. Perfect wings line their eyes, and the dark smokey makeup adds dimension where their natural features hood seductively. They always keep their midnight blue hair short on the sides, but the waves atop their head always seem to have a direct correlation to their mood. Right now, the tousled and chaotic locks—disrupted by hands running through them over and over—raise the hairs on my neck.

"Okay, let's get you settled in, little man. Your mom and I need to do something, but Ash can keep you company, and I'm sure Cy will come out of hiding if you're loud enough." They wink at him conspiratorially.

I can see the plan formulating behind Kieran's eyes as he walks away with Ash. I can't help but laugh at the mischief he will get into. I watch him climb the stairs with Ash, holding her hand.

Ember turns to me then. "Did Ash fill you in?"

"Kind of, but it sounded like there was not a whole lot to tell."

"Yeah, I think it may be better if you see for yourself."

The trepidation in their voice puts me on edge. I don't like that everyone seems to be walking on eggshells. Whatever happened, I can handle it.

"Take me to her?" I ask hesitantly.

Ember nods and we head to the stairwell. A fog of anxiety consumes the air as we rise.

When we reach the second floor, they keep going, and they lead me to an area of the building I haven't been in before. It's brighter than I expect, and as we pass the various doorways, I realize we are in their living space. I know Cy and Ember live here, but I haven't ever questioned why I have never been invited in.

What I am questioning is why I am seeing it now.

"Why didn't you take her to the med bay? It has most of the first aid supplies."

"Cy brought her up here. But we can get whatever you need from downstairs."

It strikes me as odd that Cy would choose to bring her to such a personal space, but I won't question his logic.

Ember stops outside of a doorway and looks back at me. "Go in when you're ready."

The idea that someone as seasoned with violence as Ember is telling me to prepare myself makes my stomach lurch.

What on earth is happening here?

I can't help but pause to gather myself before opening the door. I really could not have prepared for what was beyond it.

Before me lies a girl, and immediately I understand everyone's hesitation around me. It's clear why Arrick singled her out.

She looks like me.

Well, a younger version of myself. But between the blonde hair, round features, and tall frame, there is enough of a resemblance. She is me before I went through med school, residency, and childbirth.

The guilt strikes me like a hammer. The resemblance could possibly be the reason this girl endured everything she did. That she endured it at the hands of the man I escaped.

I look back at Ember and see the knowing in their eyes.

Oh, goddess. I did this to her.

If Arrick took a particular interest in her, it is definitely because of the resemblance. I know he was angry when we left, but it has only been a matter of weeks, and it is clear the man is losing control.

Someone did their best to try and care for her, but even from a short distance away, I can tell she isn't in good shape. Her skin is ashy and pale, and there are indications of trauma all over her body, and I shudder knowing who caused it.

I have to take a few deep breaths to ground myself before I can finally proceed toward her. On my approach, I have the bizarre revelation of how beautiful this woman is. Despite the injuries, she is clearly a person worthy of notice.

Refocusing, I set my bags down at the end of the bed and start to take out the supplies I will need to do an initial exam.

She is asleep, but there are some things I can do without being too invasive.

I start by taking all of the basics to establish a baseline for her: her blood pressure, temperature, and such. I write all of this down in a small notebook before turning back to Ember.

I notice Cy in the back corner. He is so still and silent I didn't even see him when I entered. He is standing vigil in the room with his arms crossed and legs spread shoulder width apart. It's a ready position; he looks as though he is anticipating a threat just as his military training prepared him for. I give him a slight dip of my chin when our eyes connect. Then I refocus on the task at hand.

"Here is a list of equipment and supplies I am going to need. Some of it should be downstairs in the med bay, but we may need to send someone out to get the other things." I say, writing as I speak. If I am right, I will have to call in a favor with a friend to get a prescription for her too.

Ember and Cy only stand there for a moment, each of their gazes slipping over to look at the girl.

"I may try and see if we can get her records too. Do we know her name?" I ask.

Cy is surprisingly the first to speak. "Juliana Morgan."

"Okay, do we know anything else?"

Ember begins to fill in the blanks. "Her friend Jay reached out to us about retrieving her from your ex." They cringe a little at the mention of the man. "She's twenty-eight and from the area, I believe. Owns a strip bar in town. I can get in touch with him and ask questions if you need me to."

"That would be great. Thanks, Ember."

Cy speaks up. "What's wrong with her?"

"Based on my preliminary exam, she has bruises on almost her entire body. Lacerations are concentrated on her torso, which someone tried to care for. But I think she has a few broken ribs. It sounds like she's having a bit of trouble breathing too. When she wakes up, I'll do a more thorough exam, but the priority is getting fluids in her and keeping her comfortable."

"She changed. In the car," Cy said, and Ember nods their head in agreement.

"What do you mean?"

Cy stares at Ember, waiting for them to explain.

"This guy handed her off to us in one piece. Helped us get out of the building, and she seemed normal or at least aware when he was there. But the second we drove off, she shut down."

"Probably the adrenaline wearing off."

Ember continues. "Not entirely. Something was going on. I kept an eye on her on our way back, and it was like she withdrew into herself. She looked empty, and then she was asleep."

"Okay. That's good to know. I will keep an eye on her when she is up." I quickly jot down a few more necessary supplies, tear out the page, and hand the list to them. "Get this, and we will go from there."

They both look reluctant to leave, and it isn't until after a silent conversation between them that Ember finally leaves.

I guess Cy will continue his watch from the corner then.

Turning to look at the girl, guilt washes over me once more. I feel beholden to her, and I silently swear I will do my best to care for the darling girl.

XVI

PAIN OF LOVE

Griffin

Arrick's unhinged when he finally comes out from his lockdown.

I walk into the main warehouse to find him surveying the damage of the day. Bricks are singed and destroyed. The acidic vinegary smell of burnt heroin permeates the air, and a layer of powder coats everything that wasn't completely destroyed by the fire.

Arrick paces about the floor with a murderous expression on his face.

The warehouse is a wreck, and everyone is doing their best to simultaneously clean up the mess and stay out of the boss's warpath.

When he's destroyed enough, he bellows out into the rafters, "How in the hell did this happen?"

Everyone is quiet, but it's expected that I will be the one to buffer his anger. Young as I am, it's my responsibility to oversee security. I'm the one to answer for this.

"Sir, we're still getting an update from those who

were on patrol. The intruders cut the security feed when they entered, and we were without surveillance during the incident."

"Griffin, thank fuck. Okay, well, tell me what we do fuckin' know then." He mumbles under his breath, "Fucking useless, all of them."

For a man with unlimited resources and riches, he really has no understanding of how his own business works. Nor does he value the people who support the whole operation.

"Damages so far seem to be contained to the warehouse. We lost a total of five men. Two were stationed at the southern entrance to the building by the garage. We found the other three in the building." I have a moment of guilt as I remember the two men I killed myself. But I remind myself it was necessary. "It appears they were making their way to the upper floors and the residence quarters."

I pause to see if he has any kind of reaction, but the control he exudes is almost more unsettling. Like a kettle heating until it screams, he stands there with his boiling rage while I give my report. Though technically I shouldn't know much of this information—I haven't talked with the men yet—but a lie is easy enough, and I can cover my tracks later.

"What else?" he asks.

"They managed to escape through the garage." I

pause in anticipation of an outburst. "And they took one of your cars to do it."

"They what?" he roars.

"They took the Aston Martin as their escape vehicle."

Then it comes, the explosion I'm anticipating.

He picks up the nearest object, which happens to be a glass beaker, and throws it across the room, where it shatters against a metal beam.

Turning to me, he growls, "What did they want? What did they take?"

I stand my ground as I reply, "Nothing as far as we can tell. They destroyed bricks of product here with a fire, but they didn't appear to take any of it, and upon a cursory search, they didn't take anything from the upper floors either. They were here, and then they weren't."

Several more beakers and various other lab equipment in the vicinity are then victims of his tantrum.

Finally seeming to have expelled the final bit of anger in him, Arrick composes himself and turns to walk out of the warehouse.

I don't want anything to do with this man anymore. The assignment no longer matters to me, and a part of me is done. But I know my obligation, and I follow the man anyway.

I can only think of Jules as we make our way back

to his office, to the room where I first laid eyes on her. When we enter, I have to suppress a wince as my eyes are drawn to the column where I found her chained. The area is clean as if no one were ever there.

I pray the people who took her away, Cy and Ember, make sure she's okay. That they really were sent by her friend, Jay. That they can be trusted.

There's an itch in me saying I won't truly ever trust anyone with Jules. I won't be satisfied until I have my eyes and hands on her. Until I'm by her side. Or at her feet.

Arrick is pacing the room. Every once in a while, his eyes glance at the column, but he never says anything about the girl he kept there.

"How did this all happen?" His anger is building as he continues. "First, that bitch ran off with my son, *my* son, and they're nowhere to be found. Now we had someone completely shut down the compound and trash the product?"

Exasperation rolls off him in thick waves, but beyond that is fearsome violence waiting to be unleashed.

Conveniently, we're interrupted.

"Sir. They finished doing inventory. Here are the reports," a man says.

Arrick scans the report and freezes at something he reads. "The other merchandise. Is this correct?"

Stupidly, the man hesitates in his answer. "The...

the merchandise? Kept in storage?"

Arrick stares at the man until he speaks.

"Yes, there's only one missing. Everyone else is secured in holding."

"Which one?" The words come through Arrick's gritted teeth, and I brace for the answer I know is coming.

"The blonde. The one Little John brought in. We can't locate her." There's sweat beading on the poor guy's forehead as he tries to hold his ground against the boss's stare.

Arrick swivels to me. "Griffin, you were the one to take her out of here. What happened to the girl." There's no question in his words.

Part of me knows this could be the end. It will take every trick I have to pull off this kind of lie. Arrick is a smart man, and he can see right through most people. It's impressive enough that I have worked my way into his trusted circle so quickly over the past four years.

"You said fuck her or kill her. I picked fuck for a couple days and then threw her back in with the rest." I keep my voice cold, but I cringe internally.

"Well, what about security footage? Something must be on there."

Hoping the confirmation the pair of strangers gave me about corrupting the existing security footage when they shut down the system was correct, I commit to the lie.

"Unfortunately, when the intruders corrupted the system, they also managed to corrupt the drives with historical footage. If someone did take her, we don't have the footage to see who it was. We could bring someone in to try and recover the files, but it will take time."

Nothing can be done to quell the man's rising anger. As he begins pacing, I look to the man on my left and motion for him to get out, and like a scared rabbit, he bolts out of the room.

Normally, the office space, if you can call it that, is cavernous and intimidating. But with the palpable emotions coming off of Arrick, it quickly becomes a stifling sauna.

"Sir." I need to proceed with caution here, but I have to keep moving.

A still target is a dead one.

"Sir," I repeat. "We do have options here. It's going to take a bit of time. I need to speak with all the men and piece together what happened. We need to identify problem areas and resolve those before we resume operations."

"No. What you need to do is find the fuckers who did this. Find my wife. Find my son. Find the girl."

My only choice at the moment is silence.

"Everything that is mine was taken from me." He

quiets as he speaks. "I won't stand to have anything else taken. Lock this place down and get shit together, Griffin. You're goin' huntin'."

"Yes, sir."

I turn to leave, but his words stop me dead in my tracks. "Did you enjoy the girl? She's a real nice piece. Reminds me of my wife. A good lay too."

If my back hadn't been to him when he spoke, everything would be ruined. Hearing him speak about Juliana, my Jules, like this, or rather at all, is too much. He has no right to touch her, talk about her, or even think about her. I want to put Arrick in his place, but it would only get me shot.

But I made a promise to her that I need to keep: to get out and find her.

Giving him no reaction, I respond, "Best I've had. But you already know that."

The words feel vile coming out of my mouth, but I hear the huff of agreement and know I've made the right call. I take the response as my cue to leave and stride evenly out of his office.

I can't alert him to anything suspicious; otherwise, we will have larger problems at hand. I can't leave the compound, but I need to get in contact with Quinn. He needs to know what happened, and if my instincts are right, I need a plan to extract myself. But that's Quinn's problem for another day. But I don't see this ending well for me if I stay.

Eventually, Arrick will start to connect dots. He probably already suspects he has a mole among the ranks. He might be erratic, but you can't accuse the man of being stupid. If I want to live to see Juliana, I need to get out soon.

The moment I close the doors to my quarters, I go to the dresser and dig around for the burner hidden there.

I quickly send an SOS text to Quinn before sitting on the bed and hanging my head in my hands.

Everything has turned to shit so quickly.

One moment I'm holding the woman of my dreams, and the next, she's gone and I'm planning my exit strategy so I can survive.

Then and there, I make a decision.

I'm done. Soon as I find her, I'm out.

When it chimes, I look at the phone for my instructions. Satisfied with Quinn's response, I go about packing a few items. Only what I can carry with me without drawing attention to myself.

Thankfully, the security system is still down. Arrick knows I'm leaving, and as long as I manage to avoid running into anyone, I should be able to meet Quinn with no problem.

Grabbing the few things I packed, I leave and make my way quietly to the compound's exit.

It's time to move on, hopefully with Jules right beside me.

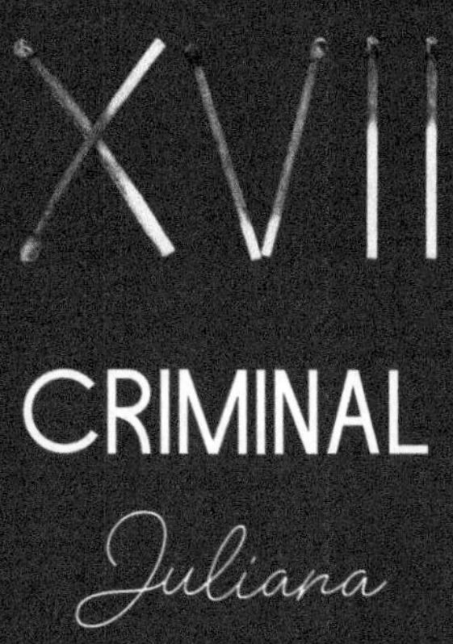

CRIMINAL

Juliana

I wake up in an unfamiliar room wearing unfamiliar clothing for the second time. I should be startled. But I immediately spot the man who brought me here. I start to relax and take in my surroundings.

I'm groggy, but the pain that became my new constant companion is duller. The next thing I am acutely aware of is the needle in my arm, which skyrockets my pulse. I start to sense the cords attached to me by sticky pads, hear the increasing beep of a machine, and finally, feel the cool touch of a hand on mine.

"Welcome back. You're safe here," a woman says.

I believe her for some reason. It's something about the voice. It's calming, like when my mom would sing me to sleep after a nightmare as a child. I try to focus on the hand and the voice to calm my racing heartbeat before opening my eyes.

Turning towards them, I brace myself for another new interaction.

Since leaving Griffin, my entire body has been on fire. It started in the car when I first felt the lack of his presence. My body began to feel hot and itchy, sounds were too loud, light was too bright, the world was too much. I retreated to the emptiness, my own little dreamland when it became too much, but some of the week's events are starting to all come back.

I hear the person speak, but don't process what they are saying. I've already retreated into the safety of my mind. I can only listen to the lullaby of their voice, not internalize the meaning of the words. They must catch on since they stop speaking.

Their hand leaves mine, and I hear retreating footsteps on the carpet as I drift back off to the emptiness where I'm secure.

Later, I am woken by the same soft voice.

"Juliana? Juliana. I need you to wake up. We need you to eat."

Dragging myself out of the void, I start to regain awareness of everything.

How do they know my name?

The soft voice is standing by my side, and the escape guy is standing in the room. Only this time, he's at the foot of my bed.

His tall stature gives him a solid presence in the room. A muscular form displays familiar tattoos across his cool dark skin, and my eye catches on the US Army insignia on his bicep. They flow with every minute movement he makes and highlight his athletic frame. I follow them up his arms and neck to his sharp jawline. He's clean cut with a short beard and perfectly faded line up hair style. But it's his angular cheek bones mirroring the piercing gaze of his hazel eyes that draw me in. The man is terrifyingly beautiful.

I roll my head towards the voice and see what most surely must be an angel. She's surrounded by light that shines through slightly greyed blonde hair, and my brain's logical side knows there must be windows to the outdoors behind her. It's pleasant to see her bathed in light like a celestial being.

"Hi, sweetheart. I'm going to reach behind you to help prop you up, okay?"

I mean to nod, but by the way her lips quirk at the corner, I must look ridiculous.

Suddenly, I'm up, and food is placed on a tray in front of me. It doesn't look like typical hospital food though, so I must not be in one.

There's pudding.

Maybe I'm wrong about the hospital thing?

"I need you to eat," she says.

I look down at the tray of food. It looks pretty appetizing, but I can't bring myself to lift my hands to grab the utensils. Everything is sluggish and heavy. My body's exhaustion has caught up with me. My movements are slowed by whatever the needle is pumping into my veins.

The voice, a woman, speaks. "How about I help you, okay?"

I turn to look at her as she settles next to me. She picks up some chicken with the fork and brings it to my lips. It's such an intimate act.

As she feeds me, I study her. She has dark sandy blonde hair and ocean blue eyes. Her face is soft, and her presence is a comfort.

We sit there for a while until I can't eat or drink anymore. I hear someone take the tray away but don't bother to look at who it was.

She's mesmerizing.

"Juliana, right?"

I manage a nod.

"I'm a doctor. Is it alright if I examine you? I did a preliminary exam when you first arrived, but I would really like to do a more thorough one. Then we can get you healed up a bit quicker. Alright?"

I nod, and she stands, revealing her tall frame, to go about her routine.

The entire time I keep my eyes on her. She asks about taking a blood draw at some point, and I guess I agree because I can feel the needle in my arm seconds later. Other than that, the exam passes in a blur. When she's done, she sits down on the edge of the bed.

"It looks like you've been through quite a lot recently. You have four broken ribs and cuts that will need to be stitched. But I think overall you're going to be okay." She smiles at me. "I'm going to leave you for a while to rest, but I'll be back soon to do your bandages."

She squeezes my hand before she gets up and leaves. I can't help but wonder where she came from.

First, Griffin found me and took care of me. Then two strangers whisked me away because Jay is searching for me. Now I have this woman's full attention as she mends my wounds and makes me whole.

When she comes back, I gather myself enough to finally speak. "What's your name?"

"Oh! Sage, my name is Sage." She smiles as she speaks, then gestures to the corner. "And the lurker over there is Cy. You've already met Ember too."

I look at Cy and find him with a stern, serious expression on his face.

What is his deal?

Our eyes connect, and there's a flash of an unidentifiable emotion that sweeps across his face.

Refocusing on Sage, I continue my questioning. "Where am I?"

She looks over at Cy before answering my question. "I'm not sure I can tell you, but know you're safe here."

"They said Jay sent them to get me. Where is he?"

"I don't know, darling. I only just got here. We can

ask Ember when they get back. In the meantime, let's get you patched up and change your bandages."

A knock at the door announces Ember's entrance.

The first thing that strikes me is their unnaturally blue hair. Its midnight hue perfectly balances their warm complexion. Everything about them seems calculated to minimize and hide their exquisite beauty. Neither masculine nor feminine, it's like their uniqueness highlights their most authentic form. They walk with a purpose, and the movements are articulated as they approach.

They direct their attention to Sage first. "How is she?"

"Well, she's awake, so how about we ask her directly, shall we?" Sage teases.

Ember's gaze locks with mine as they approach me.

"Where's Jay?" It's the concern running circles in my mind. I need to know where he is. Why isn't he here?

Sage sighs, and I feel a flame of anger ignite.

"We told him to stay away," Ember offers.

"What! Why?" I make no effort to keep my voice contained but my words are still a little sluggish.

"There is a lot of fallout happening after our exit the other day. We didn't want you going directly back to him in the case they sent someone after you. If you go to him, they'd track you down there, and we don't want to risk they'll find you. "

"That's not your call to make," I snap. "If he hired you to come get me back, then you still haven't fulfilled your agreement."

"Our contract with your friend requires us to 'acquire and ensure the safety of'... You're not getting out of here," they respond.

I stare them down.

"Call Jay. Now." My voice makes it clear this is not a request.

I hear a huff come from the corner and turn to see Cy smirking.

"Something amusing?" I spit. My anger is quickly rising. I can feel pressure building that will soon erupt into the room.

"Didn't think you had it in you, that's all."

"Excuse me? What do you mean by that?"

He shrugs, and the action makes me grit my teeth. I could strangle him.

"Didn't think you had any fight left." He shrugs, and the urge to hurt him swells.

I've never been one for violence, but something has unleashed in me recently. Anger has never really been a useful emotion in the past. I've treated it like something that can be put away or traded for something more productive my whole life. But I understand its purpose now.

Anger is a catalyst. It's an agent of change. It's fire that fuels action and gets things moving.

I'm embracing my anger and letting the feeling take hold in my body. I want to do something with it. I want to lash out in response to his cutting remarks.

"You don't know anything about me, so shut the hell up." Venom laces my words. I turn back to Ember. "Call Jay. Now."

They look taken aback but still reach for the phone and hand it to me.

I immediately start dialing for Jay. After a few rings, I hear him pick up.

"Hello?"

"Jay?" My hands start shaking, and my breaths become shallow.

"Julia? Thank goddess."

Anger morphs into a relief I didn't know I need. My body shakes, and I breathe in what feels like the first real gulp of oxygen I've taken in weeks. Something in me unravels at the sound of his voice, and I start to sob.

"Talk to me. Where are you? Are you okay? Julia, please."

The reaction rolls through me. It takes over every nerve and muscle in my body. All control is gone, and I sit there crying.

More muffled words come through the phone, but I can't understand them over my cries. Suddenly, the phone is snatched out of my hand, and I look up to see everyone in the room staring at me except for Cy. He's focused on the phone and the blur of words coming through it.

My body continues to shake as Cy takes hold of the moment. I can still hear Jay frantically trying to get answers from the other end of the line.

Cy is short and commanding when he speaks. "She's here. She's fine. Call you later."

Jay's protest begins to sound through the phone until Cy hangs up, and the room goes quiet except for my sobs.

I'm still crying uncontrollably. Any strength I had quickly fled my body when I heard Jay again.

There's a long moment with me shaking and crying in bed, and onlookers staring at me with varied expressions of concern. Except for Cy, who seems fed up. He tosses the phone on the bed and storms out of the room.

There I sit, overwhelmed, crying, and completely unsure about what the future holds. The world falls away as I cry, and my mind falls into a frenzy trying to sort out the events of the day.

Soon after, I feel my body strain, and my heartbeat slows as I sink into a deep drug induced slumber.

XVIII

BEGGIN FOR THREAD

Cy

The girl's tough; there's no denying it.

The moment we found her, I saw the strength in her. But seeing her break down in the room is the opposite of the woman she needs to be. Whatever she experienced deserves retribution, not tears.

So I leave. I don't want to witness that.

Frustration is the predominant feeling she's brought me. But the truth is, underneath the frustration lies a building attraction I desperately want to deny. For fuck's sake, I've been with my partner for over a decade. I don't need this in my life. I should be satisfied, but the fucking girl draws me in, and I feel something for her that isn't entirely welcome.

I'm making my way to our gym on the first floor, and I don't hear when Ember calls out to me over my own mumbled scolding.

Their hand on my shoulder breaks me out of my thoughts, and I turn to face them defensively.

I see it coming, but I let the punch to my shoulder land anyway. I deserve it, after all. I've been a complete ass.

Ember only confirms what I already know.

"What the hell was that?" I expect anger to lace their words, but it sounds more like pity.

I hate pity.

"Not ready to talk about it yet," I say, shrugging. I should've known better. Ember will push. They always do. Thirteen years together has taught them a lot, and they are able to see right through me.

"Cy, you don't get to go silent on me. Not about this. Tell me what's going on."

Deciding it's better to have this conversation in private, I drag them into the gym, close the door, and then stride over to the equipment cabinet.

Only silence meets me as I go about methodically wrapping my hands. Ember's patience is admirable yet vexing at times.

"Cy," Ember prompts.

"'S complicated."

"It always is with you, but whatever is going on up there needs to come out; otherwise, you'll overthink yourself into oblivion." They make their way to my side and poke me in the forehead to make their point.

"Spar with me, lòt mwatye."

I need to vent some of this, but words won't cut it,

and nothing feels better than working myself to exhaustion.

Ember follows my lead and begins wrapping their hands as I make my way to the mat.

We strive for honesty in our relationship, and I hope what I have to share won't rock us too much. I can't ever lose Ember, but I also can't ignore whatever else is building. Not that I've ever been very good with all the feelings junk.

We've always had a special balance between us. Our needs overlap where they matter. No one should ever fulfill one person's every need, and from the beginning, Ember and I have known that our relationship may extend beyond the two of us.

"I don't do this. Talkin' 'bout feelings. You know that," I say.

Centering myself as I relax into a fighting stance, I think about my next words. Clearly, Ember is done prompting. They only wait for me to continue while we circle each other.

Predictably, they make the first move, lunging at me, and I easily block the hit.

"She has me off balance."

I've never been good at reading the expressions of others or expressing myself, but Ember is more open with me than others. Understanding and relief wash through them at my words.

They try to side swipe me before we settle into a rhythm as I continue. "Feels personal."

"You feel something for her." The words are sympathetic, and I relax a little more.

"Yeah, I dunno." I take a swing, aiming for their torso, but they block me at the last second.

"Are you worried about us? Because I understand. You know how we work." The consideration they put into their words makes me appreciate my partner even more. I love what we have. I don't want to lose it. "I can see myself feeling something for her too. Not physically, but you know that."

Meeting their eyes, I drop my hands.

"What?" Their response puzzles me. The girl draws me to her, but it's a little shocking to hear Ember feels something too. They don't typically respond to new people like that. Though it's a comfort to hear. "I don't understand."

"She's special, for lack of a better word. I don't know what it is, but she feels different, right?"

"Yeah, she does." We're silent for a moment while we stand there looking at each other before I speak. "Whadda we do?"

"Who knows. But for now, we keep her safe. Eventually, we reunite her with her friend, and we go from there," they say.

"What about the other guy? The one from the compound?"

"What about him?"

"You heard 'em. Obviously something between 'em, and you heard their last conversation. The promise he made her," I say.

"We'll deal with that too when the time comes."

Their confidence in whatever plan is forming in their head settles my nerves.

I'm not normally like this; I'm the grounded one. I'm good at staying in the present moment. You have to be in our line of work.

I know I can trust Ember, but I don't like this feeling of losing control. Like there's nothing I can do.

"How's she?" I inquire.

"Well, you storming out wasn't the best way to make an exit. So that didn't really help, but Sage gave her a sedative, so she's sleeping."

"Should probably talk to her. Apologize."

"Ya think? Look, whatever is going on with you is yours to deal with. I'm always here for you. You know that..." They begin unwrapping their hands in preparation to leave. "but don't let this bleed onto Juliana. She's dealing with enough. Plus, I think Sage would strangle you. She's been mothering her."

Watching them go, I sit with my thoughts for a while before resuming my workout and venting a little more of my unwanted emotions.

Resolved to apologize for my behavior, I make my way back through the building to the room where I've put the girl. I really should have taken her to the med bay we have set up, but instead, my feet carried me towards the section where Ember and I live.

I don't allow myself to pause at the door, and I swing it wide open as I enter.

The good doctor is standing next to the bed and looks up at me with a glare before motioning for me to close the door.

I click the door shut and make my way to stand opposite the doctor. I stay there for a moment before I can bring myself to speak.

"Sorry," I say. The statement is clear, but the doctor looks at me skeptically.

"It's not me you need to apologize to." When the woman turns to look at the girl lying in bed, her face softens from its previously hard state. "She noticed, you know."

Which puzzles me. The idea that the girl clocked my earlier departure while in such a state of distress is confusing, to say the least.

"What?"

"When you left, she noticed. You took something

away from her that she needed right then. Of course she noticed when you stormed off." She takes a breath in an attempt to collect herself. "She was so worked up I was forced to sedate her. I was afraid she would hurt herself."

"Shit," I murmur.

"I have an idea of what happened to her, but there's no way to tell the full extent of it or how she's going to respond when she starts to come back to herself, okay? So you need to check yourself before she gets hurt because you're being a reckless fool."

My second scolding within the hour is not doing any favors for my ego, but I know it's well deserved. I try to ignore the doctor's words as I stare down at the girl. She looks so peaceful sleeping there. Her blonde hair, pale skin, and round lips draw me in like a masterwork at a museum. Her curves and pillowy breasts make me want to sink into her. I'm used to mechanics and machinery and the practiced motions of combat. But this girl is pure art.

Ember is right. There is something about her. It draws you in and keeps you captive. Even while sleeping.

Looking up at the doctor, it appears she has been studying me. I don't like the look in her eyes. There is too much knowledge there. I don't notice my walls dropping, but she must have. It feels invasive to have her look at me like that. The idea that she may see more than I want causes me to slam my walls up and reset the mask I wear.

"How long 'til she's up?" My attempt at redirecting the conversation is obvious, but the doctor graciously lets me win the small battle.

"Probably another couple of hours until the sedative wears off. But we will have to watch her carefully when she does."

"And how long until she's up and moving?"

"Well, it depends."

"On?"

The doctor's sigh only carries a small hint of her annoyance. Ember is better at this. The whole people thing. I should have left them to deal with this. But I need to apologize to the girl.

"How quickly her wounds heal and bones mend. How much we're able to get her to eat and drink. There's a lot going into all of this. She's not going to jump out of bed the second she wakes up. My best guess? Six to eight weeks."

I scoff at that. Sure, the doctor would be paying attention to all of the medical stuff. But something tells me this girl would be the first one pushing to get out of bed. She doesn't strike me as someone who sits still well.

The doctor sends me another one of those looks silently saying she thinks I am unraveling, but I ignore her and instead focus on the girl.

So many people have failed her up to this point; I won't let myself be one of those failures.

Resigned to waiting for her to wake up, I position myself back in the corner where I previously stood and resume my vigil.

As I wait for her to wake up, Ember brings me a couple sidearms and a few knives to clean each time they visit but never question why I stay. Annoying as it is at first, the doctor keeps bringing food and forcing us all to eat. I nearly bite her head off at the suggestion of resting though.

The more time that passes, the more I begin to worry. Which is an unwelcome and uncomfortable feeling, in my opinion.

Of course it's one of the rare moments when I'm alone with her when she begins to stir. I check the hallway for Ember or the doctor, but they are nowhere to be found.

With no one else around, I concede to my desire to be near her and approach her side. I still maintain a distance from her as though coming too close would also inflict harm on me. But any illness I experience around this girl would likely be one of the heart, not the body or mind.

I don't know how long I stand there looking at her,

but when she finally looks at me, I feel the ricochet of the fissure running through my internal walls. I cling to them in a desperate attempt to keep them up, but a part of me wants to let them crumble for her. Like they did for Ember all those years ago.

She remains relaxed as she looks up at me, and her content expression eases some of the bitter feelings I've accrued.

"I should get the doctor." The words fumble out, and I cringe at the sound of my voice.

Before she can respond, I walk out of the room to find someone else to deal with the girl.

Relief is quick when I spot Ember and the doctor turn the corner, walking towards me.

Though they're still far away, I can't help but call out to them, "She's awake."

They look at each other briefly and make their way to join me. I hang back a little and follow them into the room where the girl is sitting with a look of confusion and shock combined.

The doctor breaks the tension by speaking first. "We heard you were up. How are you feeling?"

Her response is slow. "Tired."

"Completely understandable. Your body is dealing with a lot, and it will take a while before you can resume normal activities." The doctor hesitates before continuing. "And there's probably more needed to be done other than patching you up.”

"Really? You think so?”

I huff at her response. At least the girl still owns a sense of humor. The sound draws her attention, and her eyes narrow at me.

"You.”

Ember moves forward a bit as if to protect me from the girl. But I don't need their protection. If anything, the girl needs protection from me. I'm definitely the more lethal of the two of us. Though the stare she's giving me might make me doubt I would prevail so easily if she wasn't injured.

"Me." My lips quirk at the corner.

Quickly playing the mediator, Ember jumps in before I fuck things up further.

"How about we concentrate on getting you better," they say, turning to the doctor for direction.

"Well, wounds such as yours typically take a month or two to heal. Should things continue to progress well, I think we can have you out of bed in the next few weeks.”

Hope returns to the girl at the doctor's words.

"So I can leave soon then. Go back home," she says.

"No," I snap out.

The hope drains from her face and is quickly replaced with anger as her head whips to look at me. She remains silent. Glaring at me.

"What Cy means to say..." Ember cuts in. "There's still a concern for your safety, and it's not a good idea to resume your normal life."

The doctor interjects next. "And while you may be physically patched up, you will likely need physical therapy to help you get back your strength and range of motion."

"Training too. So this shit doesn't happen again." Everyone seems shocked when I speak. Either for the simple fact that I'm engaging in the conversation or for recommending she train. Who the fuck knows.

Most of all, the girl looks stunned, as though it's unfathomable that I might give a fuck. Which, maybe it is considering how much of an ass I've been up to this point.

"Okay," the doctor speaks slowly. "Maybe training too. But only when you're well enough."

With that, I mentally withdraw from the conversation. At the sound of Ember's voice, I am forced to rejoin the group.

"Earth to Cy," they say. I look up. "Since you're all gung-ho about getting Juliana on her feet for training, why don't you take over her physical therapy in the meantime?"

I look at them quizzically, and the doctor answers my implied question. "We can't take her to any legitimate practitioners."

"It's too much exposure and too many questions, and you're the D1 athlete of the group." Ember adds.

"We need someone we trust to help," the doctor says.

I narrow my eyes at them. They're up to something, but I don't know what it is.

"Fine." And I finally leave altogether.

I CAN'T BREATHE

Juliana

For weeks upon weeks, I go through the torture routine Cy creates for me. Every morning, he has me up at six to begin the day with whatever punishment fits his fancy, and he isn't one to let up no matter how much I complain. Cy definitely knows how to push a person to their limit.

In the beginning, someone was constantly with us. He went easier on me then. Especially since I could really only handle minimal PT. We began with getting my mobility and stamina back. But when Sage gave the okay that Cy could start my "training" after her promised six weeks, Sage and Ember stopped hanging around. That's when the real torment began.

We've been at it for a week and surprisingly, combat training is easier to adapt to than physical therapy. It's a lot like the years I spent in a dance studio. The purpose is different, but the foundations are similar enough, and my body finally starts to feel comfortable with the routine.

Sage and Kieran are over every day and we all eat together almost every evening. Cy even made a gluten free roux for his Gramma M's jambalaya recipe, which is the most outright kindness I think he's shown me. Kieran and Ember are working on a project together. It's either a computer game involving robots or a robot for a computer game. Nothing they say about it makes sense to me. Although Kieran's excitement about the project and Ember's proud look whenever he gets going is entertaining enough that we all let him ramble on about it.

The kid is absolutely adorable, and it's nice having someone around who still has the innocence of a child. I mean, he is a child, but it's nice nonetheless. His is the only genuine smile I see during the day. I need his joy more than he will ever know.

I think it's why Sage started bringing him every day. Maybe even why they are here at all. She doesn't really need to check in on me anymore. But the two show up every morning right after breakfast. Kieran tears through the hallways until he finds Ember, who picks him up, tosses him in the air, and ruffles his sandy hair when they set him down.

Kieran's adamant he is far too old and mature for any of this, but I can tell he loves the attention. Little boys never really want affection to stop. That only happens when they start to learn how society expects them to repress their emotions and "act like a man." Having them both here is a good thing. After they leave, everything gets quiet, and I'm left alone.

It doesn't take long to figure out that Cy and Ember are in a relationship. A unique one, just like the two of them. They have a connection based on something beyond sexual attraction. The strength of it is made evident in both the length of their relationship and the comfort they have with each other.

Between the two of them, Ember makes an effort on occasion to keep me entertained, but Cy avoids me. Unless he is putting me through my own circle of hell. I have his undivided attention then. He meticulously studies every move I make and analyzes for flaws. But he isn't looking to cut me down. He's looking for weaknesses. It's like he's trying to keep me safe in his own way.

Despite this, I still can't figure out the gruff exterior and asshole behavior he maintains around me. So it's shocking when one morning we don't immediately start with training exercises.

"I..." He chews on his words. "I should apologize."

Is Cy trying to have a heart-to-heart?

"Oh?"

"Yeah..." Clearly, he is having difficulty getting the words out. "I've been a bit of an ass."

Well, that's a double whammy. Impressive.

"I mean… based on how you've been towards me for the past two months? Yeah, I'd say you have been." When he steps towards me, I tense up. We are so close to each other. Too close for comfort, and yet somehow not close enough.

I huff out a half laugh. "I'm genuinely surprised to find out you have a heart at this point. If I didn't know better… You care about Ember, clearly. So there must be some kind of heart under your asshole exterior."

My words are sarcastic, but there is a little bit of honesty in them too. I know I am being a bitch, but it feels good to rant at him. I've been cooped up for too long. I want my real life back. My anger and resentment build every day that I'm here. Each day I'm here is another day closer to me storming out. So yeah, my anger is misplaced. It belongs to another, but he's not here.

"Not that I don't feel anything. Just prefer not to," he says.

There is almost a kind manner about him today. I wonder what prompted this. Then he steps back to put space between us and lets go of my hands. I didn't even notice when he reached for me.

"Why bring this up? We've been doing fine."

He sighs in defeat. "I promised Ember I would try harder. Figured an apology was as good a place as any to start."

"Okay. Well, that's over. Can we get back to your torture regimen?"

Laughing at my words, he turns towards the mats. A glimpse of a smile crosses his face, and it's breathtaking. Then it's like a switch flips, and Cy is immediately back to his normal self. Maybe he's a bit more relaxed?

"Get down. Stretch out. Don't want you gettin' injured. Doc would kill me."

Was that an attempt at a humor?

"Probably... Sage gives off that vibe," I say.

When I'm settled on the mat, he kneels in front of me. I notice hesitation when he reaches to touch me this time.

It's comforting to have his hands on me. Every bit of contact so far is professional, but this small moment of intimacy is proof Cy is more than his hard exterior.

It's probably his apology affecting me.

He guides my body into different positions to help loosen up my muscles, and we settle into a comfortable silence. At one point, he's leaning over me to add to the stretch, and he turns his face away from me completely. Like it's too much to look at me while our bodies are so close together. There is a new tension there neither of us want to acknowledge. Or at least there is on my part.

When we finish the warm-up, I remember how

alone we are in the room.

He coughs as he helps me up, and our hands linger, entwined together for longer than appropriate.

"Let's start with combinations," he says, shaking himself.

We work in silence as we go through all of the patterns and movements he's taught me. Relaxing into the routine gives my mind time to wander. Never a good thing.

Cy makes a swing, and I fail to block the sharp punch. It connects with my ribs, and a particular memory floods back.

I am back in the room. That feeling of sliding in and out of consciousness brings terror to the front of my mind. All I can see is his face. The man who bound me, gagged me, and gave me all of the scars that mar my skin. His face haunts me at night, but I'm normally able to avoid the memories during the day.

The sudden onslaught of images and sensations drags me into the memory further. Hands reach for me, and I react. Muscle memory from all of Cy's training kicks in, and I bend the reaching limb behind my attacker's back. My other hand reaches around to lock their head in place.

I hear them struggling to speak, but I am too deep into my memories of the past to understand. The desire to take back control is overwhelming. I want to hurt him. I want him to feel the same pain he made me go through.

Tapping on the arm wrapped around them brings me back to the present. As soon as I realize who I have in my arms, I let go and back away.

Looking at my hands, I realize what happened. I can feel tears running down my face. I am sobbing. Breathing is difficult. I began gasping for air, but it's too thick to take any in.

Then Cy is present at my back, and his arms reach to wrap around me. I fight, but he has an unrelenting grip. Struggling until my body gives out, I collapse into his arms. We sit there together, my body cradled in his. I cry while Cy does his best to comfort me.

I feel drained, but eventually my breathing returns to normal, and I find myself able to focus.

Cy's grip loosens, and he moves out from behind me, still staying in contact with me. His hand rests on my arm and makes small strokes up and down. The motion is soothing, and I need comfort, but I would never admit it to him.

"Look at me." The softness in his voice makes me look up. "That. That panic? It can't happen. You know that, right? In here, you're safe. Out there? You have to push past it."

The logical side of me understands where he's coming from, but my anger flashes at his words.

I can't control my reaction.

Can I?

How on earth am I supposed to prevent something I don't know is coming?

He must have seen right through me because his words mirror my thoughts.

"If you don't know when it's happening, we work on figurin' out what comes before." I would laugh at him if I had the energy. "Look, everyone's got something haunting 'em. We all got a bit of darkness in us. The angel and the devil sit on our shoulders waiting for us to make a decision. No right or wrong one. But you gotta make one. Pick which one you wanna feed. 'ight?"

His words are surprisingly insightful for someone generally standoffish and silently menacing. As I process, he stands and helps me to my feet. He lifts my hand, still engulfed in his, and places the most tender kiss on my inner wrist before he turns to leave.

In the space by myself, I struggle with his words and actions.

I should want to feed the angel, right?

Why does it feel like the devil is calling my name?

After washing away the events and feelings of the morning, I redress in a pair of spandex shorts and a hoodie—Ash did a little shopping for me. I'm still drained, and all I want is to curl up into a ball in my bedroom, but my stomach has other ideas.

Voices grow louder as I make my way towards the kitchen. They aren't whispering per se, but the conversation is tense and hushed.

I find Cy talking to Ember and Sage, with Kieran sitting at the kitchen table with his headphones on. The three turn to me, and their conversation abruptly comes to a halt.

"Don't mind me," I say.

Cy's stare is intense, any tenderness from earlier gone, while the others are concerned.

Of course, his response is to leave the room. I hate how he acts like he wants nothing to do with me. But then I think back to this morning and how tender he was.

Ember jumps in to fill the silence. "Hey, how ya feeling? Cy said you had a rough morning." They look like they would rather die than talk to me about this.

I groan. Of course Cy told the others. There's absolutely no privacy in this place.

I'm grateful they took me in and gave me a place to stay. Sage spent so much time putting the pieces of me back together, but I am tired of feeling like a burden. I want to return to how things were before all of this.

I want to see Jay. I miss him. He's my person. The

one I turn to when things get hard. I didn't realize how much I rely on him. Being separated from him is really starting to wear on me.

To my knowledge, the one brief phone call Cy abruptly ended is the last time any of us had contact with him. There are so many things I'm kept in the dark about. I'm getting sick of it.

"Yeah. I'll be fine," I say. Thinking a moment longer, I realized this would be the perfect time to push to see Jay. "I think..." I take a breath. "I need to see Jay."

Ember's response is immediate. "No."

I can already tell this is going to be a tense conversation. More so than whatever the trio was talking about before I joined them in the kitchen.

"I've been here for months. Has anything even happened while I've been here?" My words are met with hard stares and silence. "Look, I appreciate you trying to keep me safe, but I'm on edgecooped up in here. You haven't even let me talk to him, and I know he's probably an anxious wreck too."

Knowing she is my best bet, I turn to Sage.

"Please. I need this," I plead.

She sighs and turns to look at Ember. Something sparks in my chest, and I'm hoping she'll take my side.

"We can't know for sure they're not still looking for you," Ember reasons.

"Okay, well, there has to be some way. I don't have

to go to the club. There has to be a way you can control things, right?"

Sage and Ember sit there looking at each other.

"If you can't, I'll sneak out myself," I mutter.

This seems to get their attention, and the sigh Ember lets out is telling. They are going to cave, thank goddess.

"I make no promises, but I'll talk with Cy and try to figure out something. If we can make it work, I'll get in touch with him. But no promises," they say.

"Thank you." Joy flutters through me, but I contain my reaction.

Sage looks sympathetic, but soon her attention is drawn back to Kieran. Once Ember leaves the room, I go to sit with the two of them.

"Do you disagree?"

"What, with letting you see your friend? Of course not. But it doesn't mean I'll stop worrying." I don't respond, so I wait for her. "It comes with being a mom, I guess. You worry about your family," she says.

It isn't that I didn't know she cared about me, but it still surprises me to hear her say it out loud.

Family?

I watch as they work on Kieran's project. I know normal is relative. I know family isn't only the people you're related to by blood. Sage and Kieran have made a place for themselves in my routine and life. Even Ember and Cy have scraped out a space. And I hold out hope that I'll see Griffin again. I know things will have changed with Jay too. But I hope things won't change too much.

Part of me wants to put all of this behind me.

I'm being pulled in two different directions and I don't know where either lead. Something tells me that my road won't be paved with good intentions.

DEVIL INSIDE

Jay

I t's been months since the cops have given me any kind of update on Juliana, which doesn't really matter in the end because I know where she is, kind of.

I'm grateful for the call from Ember earlier when they told me they found her and brought her to a safe location. But it eats at me to know she's been alone with these strangers for months now.

The call from Julia all that time ago truly rocked me to my core. Hearing her in distress was agony. I've hoped she's okay with every fiber of my being, but hearing her break down nearly short-circuited me. I'm going to kill whoever ended the call so abruptly.

And now I know I can follow through.

Evidently, vengeance has been on my mind recently. I got retribution from the scumbag who took her, but the list of people who deserve my anger is quickly growing. Whoever hurt her enough to call in a doctor is at the top of the list. And to an extent, the people who are with her are up there too. It doesn't matter that they're right to make me stay away. I'm angry, and it fuels every choice I make.

It makes sense to keep my distance. It's worth the discomfort, even if it minimizes the risk of someone finding her by the smallest fraction. But I can't help but feel I should be there with her.

During the months of waiting, the only thing to do is to continue with life as normally as possible, which means running the club and making sure everything's ready for Julia when she comes home. Because she will be coming home.

Lately, I've been spending a lot more time experimenting with some of my darker inclinations; turns out I have an affinity for torture and lies.

Rosie is quickly gaining a reputation among those in the underworld as a person who can make things happen. She seems to know the right person for whatever you need done. So much so, people are seeking her out. So when someone first approached her about needing information from an uncooperative individual, she asked me.

Friends do help friends, after all.

I've never been squeamish around blood, but it's surprisingly easy to get what I want without breaking skin. I guess my dual theater and psych degrees are finally paying off. The rest of it is for my own enjoyment.

I've changed since Julia was taken. The club isn't enough to keep me occupied, and I need another way to process. I need to do something with the energy refusing to diminish. But here I am, going through the motions: reviewing payroll, paying bills, and reviewing contracts with vendors. The days drag on and blur together. Only broken up by those few moments of red.

When a stranger walks into my office, I am taken aback. It's unexpected, and my stomach twists at their appearance. I would prefer not to deal with more dramatic events if I can avoid them.

They quietly shut the door of Julia's office and move to the chair before me. Their posture is relaxed, while I am on edge.

"We have a problem." Their voice betrays the calm exterior they display.

Based on their voice alone, I decide—this must be Ember. And this can't be anything good. I'm not sure I'm ready to hear whatever they have to share. "How is she?"

"Oh, yeah. She's fine. Doing a lot better."

The answer is unsatisfying, but I hesitate to push for more. I don't want to cut off my only tie to Julia because I'm following my impulses rather than rational thought. I haven't heard anything for weeks. I need this.

"She's been pushing hard for you to come to visit.

Won't shut up about it," they say.

That sounds more like the Julia I know. Not the tearful woman I listened to over the phone.

"What did she threaten?"

They let out a small laugh. "How'd you know?"

"She's my best friend." I shrug.

They look at me for a while, and I know they can see what I'm not willing to say out loud. Not yet, anyway. Especially not to anyone other than Julia.

"She's threatening to sneak out on her own. Thought we should take that seriously."

"Probably for the best." My words are selfish. "And?"

"Well, things have been pretty silent for the past few weeks. We figure maybe it's time for us to complete the job."

I push out a heavy breath before relaxing into the chair. "She gets to come home?"

"Not exactly. You told us to retrieve her and make sure she's safe." The reminder makes my anger at them resurface. Even knowing I'm the one who made the original decision. "We're less concerned about an im-mediate threat, but to be on the safe side, it would be best to take you to her."

I lean forward eagerly and place my clasped hands on the desk. "Tell me when and where. I'll be there."

Ember smirks knowingly before continuing.

"Thought you'd say that. Meet me here," they say

and slide a paper across the desktop. "In three days at five thirty. End of the workday means more people to disappear into."

I hear the words, but I'm fixed on the address in my hands. This is my chance to go to her. By the time I look up, they are gone.

The rest of the day passes uneventfully after Ember's departure, and everything continues as normal until my phone rings.

"Hello?"

"Jay. This is Detective Bacon."

I sigh inwardly. There's nothing they can tell me that I don't already know. Ember was here only hours ago. And I'm definitely not going to share any of that with the police. I've told them everything they need to know. The rest of it is unnecessary.

"I have an update on your friend's case." Silence comes over the phone, and I guess she's expecting some kind of response. "Unfortunately, we are going to have to close this case. I know it's disappointing, but we don't have the resources to keep this going."

I should protest, but I don't have the energy anymore. I guess the detective interprets my silence as a shock because she continues.

"If it makes you feel any better, there is one officer

who won't let go for some reason."

Well, that is new.

"Do you know what he wants?" I ask tentatively.

"He's in a different task force and thinks your friend's disappearance is somehow connected to his case. So he's pushing for every lead he can. Don't be surprised if he reaches out to you or shows up on your doorstep." The pause coming through the phone means nothing good for sure. "But keep your phone on you. An eye out. That's all."

"Okay, thanks for the warning?"

"Yeah, sure. No problem." Then the line goes dead.

I get the call a few days later, only hours before I'm supposed to meet Ember.

"This is Jay."

"Hi, Jay. I'm Officer Reyes with HPD. I know officially your friend's case is closed, but I was hoping to talk with you about Juliana's disappearance."

The way he says her name makes me pay attention. It's so casual. As if he knows her personally, but there is no way he could.

"I was hoping to meet with you today. Maybe at a coffee shop or something. Wherever works for you really," he says.

His eagerness strikes me as odd, but I don't really want to drag the charade on anymore. I know it looks odd if I suddenly stop being invested. My only option is to play along.

"Sure, I'm at the club, but there's a cafe nearby where we can go."

"Yeah, of course. I'll be there as soon as I can."

I hang up and go find Rosie to hold down the fort for me. "I'm going out. I have a thing."

"A thing?" She quirks her eyebrow at me.

"Yeah." She is clearly not letting go of this until I give her more. "There's a cop who's still asking questions about Julia. I'm meeting him for coffee to get him to go away."

"I'm coming with you."

Her response is immediate but not altogether surprising. She's been with me every step of the way and somehow makes things happen I can never fathom. I can't tell her no at this point, but I wish I hadn't dragged her into this with me. She should get to live a normal life. She doesn't need this shit.

"Jay, I'm coming with you. You're not going without someone to watch your back. If it makes you feel better, I'll hang back and keep an eye on things. Kay?"

Satisfied with the plan, we make our way to the car and drive to meet the officer.

I hang back while Rosie goes inside, but I immediately spot the officer upon entering as there don't appear to be any other men here. There's something about him that screams protector. He looks like he straddles the line separating the bad guys from the good. Between his toned body and tattoos, you know he is a physically powerful man. But dressed in washed-out jeans, a faded T-shirt, boots, and a beaten-up jacket, he also gives off an endearing energy. When I approach, he stands and holds out his hand. I notice how tall he is, but looking up at him doesn't put the fear of goddess in you. More like he is your guard or knight from some fairy tale, ready to protect and serve.

I try to keep my body loose, but I want this over as fast as possible. I try to calm my thoughts by reminding myself this isn't any different from every one of my conversations with the police so far.

I'm not going to learn anything new from him. I'll stick to the narrative. There's no need to add any additional details. He's another cop asking the same questions we've been over before.

Only it's not how the conversation starts.

"Hi, thanks for meeting me," he says. The rapid pace of his words has me on alert. There's definitely something going on with this guy. It's only a matter of figuring out what. "I learned about Jules's case, and I want to help if I can. I know they closed the case, but if she's still missing, then someone should be looking."

Shock ricochets through me. This is a lot more than general interest, and I have a feeling this conversation is not going to go how I expected.

"Yeah, Detective Bacon called me earlier this week to give me the news." I keep my reply short.

"It's bullshit and politics. I want to help... if I can."

"I've already told the police everything I know."

"I know. I just... I want to know more about her. Maybe if I have a better feel of who she is, then tracking her down will be easier." His response seems thoughtful in an almost personal way.

Over his shoulder, I finally spot Rosie, who has angled her body more in our direction. Something must have piqued her interest as well.

I contemplate his request and decide there is no harm in telling him more about Juliana. I share about how we met in school and the business we built together. He asks questions about what kind of person she is, her character and morals.

As we talk, he visibly relaxes. As though hearing about her is a comfort. Which is an absurd idea. When I begin telling him about the kidnapping, he's right back to being a cop. But again, everything he asks only covers the same information already in the reports a thousand times over.

"I appreciate you meeting me. I know this must feel endless, but I want to help. I want to get her back home and make sure she's okay, that's all," he says.

His words aren't those of an objective outsider. It sounds personal. There's no way they know each other. If they did, then I would know about him too, right?

I sit there with my cold coffee as the man collects his things and says goodbye. But I barely register his departure before Rosie slides into his place.

"I don't think I was the only one listening in on you, Jay," she whispers. The words are confident with a hint of wary concern. "There was a young guy nearby that came in after you. He sat there drinking a coffee while you talked. But he wasn't on a computer or his phone. He didn't have a book or newspaper. He just kind of sat there. I couldn't see his face though, and he left before you finished up."

I only stare at her while processing the information.

We both became more aware of oddities since all this started. It's more necessary to keep track of details and people. Rosie is excellent at it. Me? Not so much. I didn't notice the guy at all. But the fact he was here is concerning.

Or it could be nothing.

I look down at my coffee and see a card placed

there. Vaguely I recall the cop, Griffin, giving it to me and mentioning he wrote his direct number, which I still think is pointless. I pocket the card anyway.

"We need to go back to the club. Now," I say.

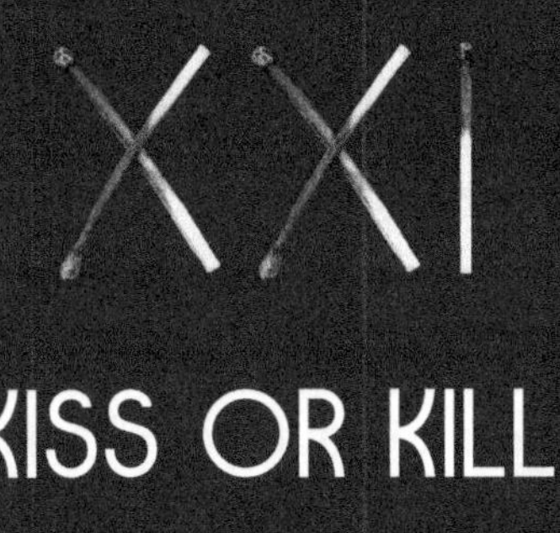

KISS OR KILL

Juliana

I almost don't believe it when Cy says they are arranging to bring Jay here. Cy isn't a person to give in so easily. If anything, all the time I've spent with him taught me he is as serious as he is lethal. But the relief I feel when he finally listens is a welcome change.

Over the past weeks, I've learned to trust these people. Sage has taken care of me more attentively than any doctor, nurse, or even parent ever has. Cy builds me up and makes me feel strong. Ember is still a bit of a mystery, but they're ready to step in when you need them.

I think they realize how much I need this though. It's one thing to be surrounded by supportive people, but I need my best friend back. I miss my home, my dog, the club. Normalcy in general. Knowing I can't go back to my life makes me anxious. I need the comfort of routine and familiarity. So much is out of my control, and I feel powerless.

They'll make it happen. They don't tell me anything beyond that. No date or time. Nothing for me to cling to other than a small sliver of hope from a half promise.

So when Cy storms into my room grumbling, with arms full of baggage, I am taken aback.

"What's all of this?" I ask.

"Picked up your friend. Evidently you're moving in with all the crap he brought."

"Jay's here?"

"Yeah. Brought some dog too."

I'm up and off the bed before he can finish the sentence.

Turning out of my bedroom, I race down the hallway towards the main living areas, hoping it's where I will find them.

I still hate running.

Sure enough, I reach the living room as Jay walks into the space. I freeze in place at the sight of him.

Paws on my thigh redirect my attention, and I look down to find Spencer bouncing in circles and jumping up to greet me. I fall to my knees and embrace him. He peppers puppy kisses across my face while wriggling out of control.

I don't notice I'm crying until a hand brushes away the tears. Looking up, I meet Jay's gaze full-on, and the tears come harder. His hair is longer, and his face looks tired. Shadows live under his eyes like he's haunted by ghosts. This is not the man I left, and the reminder shatters me.

He wraps me up in a tight embrace. We don't pull apart until we hear Kieran cry out.

"Is that a dog?!" He runs over, sliding to his knees with us.

I let go of Spencer in time for Kieran to crash into us, scoop him up, and bury his face in soft fur.

Seeing Kieran and my fur baby together brings a smile to my face. I chuckle to myself and try to breathe through the combination of tears and hiccupping laughter. The boy has clearly claimed Spence as his own, which adds a necessary levity to the moment. I'm completely overwhelmed, but I'd take these feelings over the emptiness that has consumed me for months.

"What's his name?" Kieran has a sparkle in his eyes. He gets the same one whenever he talks about his special interests like the project he and Ember are working on. The two are going to be trouble.

"His name is Spencer or Spence," I say.

Kieran adopts the slightly higher voice everyone uses with babies and cute animals. "Hi, Spencer! Can I call you Spency?"

My heart swells for the two when newly nicknamed Spency gives Kieran a big kiss on the nose. Immediately, peals of laughter fill the room.

"Alright, Kieran. Let's give them a little bit of space."

Sage's voice comes from across the room.

We must be quite the scene. All of us on the floor, Kieran holding his new best friend, me holding mine with tears streaming down my face while laughing out of control, and Jay trying his best to hold it together.

"It's alright, Sage. Spencer loves making new friends." I wink at Kieran as I speak through my tears, and a grin widens across his face.

It's then I realize how close Jay and I are sitting. How his hand rests on my arm with his thumb passing gently back and forth over my skin. It's like he can't bear not to touch me.

There's been a natural balance in our relationship since the beginning. We met back in college, and everything seemed to fall into place. There was once back then when we fooled around, and not even that made a dent in our friendship like everyone expected.

But this touch is possessive and tender, and I feel something new emerging.

Jay helps me stand while Sage makes her way over to us.

She sticks out her hand to greet Jay, and he meets her with his right hand. Which makes me aware of our hands clasping together. I look to Jay as Sage introduces herself and see a solidness to him. The set of his jaw has changed, and there's a steel to him that wasn't there before. They mirror the harsher calluses I felt on his hands.

I wonder what changes he sees with me.

"Sage. It's nice to meet you, Jay," she greets.

"Same." He looks at me, and we lock eyes. "Thanks for taking care of her."

"Of course. I'm glad you are finally able to be together."

Something about the phrasing of Sage's words makes Jay tense up, but we are interrupted by the entrance of Ember and Cy before I can overthink anything.

"Emmy!" Kieran jumps up from the ground and races to them, with Spencer close on his heels. "You have to meet Spency."

"I'm guessing this is him?" They muse.

"Yeah. He's my new best friend." Seeming to realize what he said, his face goes blank. "Sorry."

Ember reaches to ruffle the kid's hair. "That's alright, bud. You can have more than one bestie."

"Really?"

"Of course, you can, Kieran," Sage affirms, but there is a sad look in her eye.

I have a feeling Kieran doesn't really have many friends. Plus, with what little I gather about their life before whatever brought them here, I have a feeling he wasn't ever in a position to make friends in the first place.

"Ay, tèt zozo. Got anymore krap pou fi ou?"

Ember lets out something between a cough and a choke at Cy's words. Jay stares at him for a moment. Probably trying to figure out what the man said.

"Anything else you brought with you, Jay?" Ember offers. Something tells me it is definitely a paraphrasing.

"Oh, no." He turns to Kieran. "Hey, Kieran. Wanna keep an eye on Spencer for us?" I swoon internally at his use of "us."

"Can I, Mom? At least until I have to leave for camp?" The energy in Kieran's words is infectious.

"If it's alright with Juliana, then it's fine with me," Sage confirms. Her son's grin widens rapidly.

"You sure you can handle it? He can be a handful." I eye him carefully.

"I promise I'll take good care of him." Children have the most altruistic honesty about them.

I squeeze Jay's hand and tug him after me. "Let's go to my room."

"*My* room, is it?"

I pause to think about it before responding. "I guess so. I've been here long enough."

The way he looks at me with such understanding and patience rattles me.

Goddess, I missed him.

Strangely, I hesitate at the door to my room. It feels so weird to bring Jay here. So much has happened he has missed out on.

Not that I would want to push any of what happened on to him, but there is so much he doesn't know. That he wasn't there for. It makes me realize how inseparable we've been over the years. It doesn't feel right to have some part of me he doesn't know.

Pushing the thoughts away, I open the door and step through.

After our months apart, it feels odd to be alone with him. I can feel his presence by the door, but I can't face him now for some reason. I go over to the bags tossed by Cy on the bed to unpack whatever Jay brought for me.

The silence between us is brutal. I don't know where to start.

My breath releases as I hear Jay clear his throat.

"So…" He pauses. "How are you?"

That gets me to turn around and face him. I am astonished.

"Sorry. That was stupid. It sounds like something you say to an ex when you run into them at a restaurant." There is a slight chuckle in his tone, but I know we both feel the tension behind the humor.

"This is weird, right?"

"Kinda." I can see him thinking hard. "I don't know where to start. I don't think we've ever been apart for such a long time."

"Yeah. You're right." My gaze drops to my hands. I can't bear looking at him. Which is a different kind of discomfort.

I startle when Jay's finger comes underneath my chin to raise my face to him. I didn't even notice him walk towards me.

"I missed you. So much," he says.

The look he gives me brings tears to my eyes.

"Hey. Don't cry. I think we've done enough of that."

Which, of course, is the exact wrong thing to say. It's like telling a woman to calm down when she has every right to express her anger. So the tears start falling.

Both of his hands come up to cradle my face and wipe away the tears. Then he places the most delicate kiss on my forehead.

I want to tell him everything, but I don't know where to start. It feels like if I start at the beginning, I will fall apart.

I was in this state of nothingness for weeks. I can't talk about what happened with anyone. Partially because it's too painful. But mostly, I don't remember. Something broke in me. Huge chunks of time were stolen from me.

My *life* was stolen from me.

How do you tell someone you can't remember the worst experience of your life? How do you explain you're broken? That because of it, you'll never feel safe.

My best friend sees straight through me as always.

"You don't have to tell me. I'll be here to listen, but I don't need to know. A selfish part of me wants to hear everything, but you don't have to tell me anything because you think it will make *me* feel better." He presses another kiss to my temple, and I melt into the security he offers. "Kay?"

"Yeah."

The sigh he lets out next makes me tense though.

"But I do need to tell you something," he says.

Taking me by the hand, he leads me over to the bed. He drops my hand to make his way to the center but reaches back for me when I don't follow.

"I need confessional to get this out, okay?"

The worry rising in my chest stills.

This was our thing since early in our friendship. The first time, shortly after we met, Jay found out my girlfriend at the time was cheating on me. He asked to come over to my apartment but spent ten minutes pacing in the living room. When I finally convinced him to sit down, he instinctively pulled me into him, with my back against his chest. Evidently, his Catholic upbringing makes giving bad news a lot easier if you don't have to look at the person.

Since then, we've dealt with a lot of the big bad stuff like this, with me wrapped in my best friend's arms. One of the few places I feel truly safe. I settle into his arms, with my head resting against his neck, and feel the deep breath he takes.

"What happened?" The shake of my voice gave away the nerves making my pulse race.

"When you went missing... I kind of lost it."

"Kind of?"

"I think Rosie would probably say I was unhinged. Like Harley-Quinn's-revenge-on-The-Joker level of lost it." The chuckle he lets out sounds slightly pained, but he keeps going. "We reported you missing as soon as we saw the security tapes. Handing things over to the police ended up being pretty useless though. Well, the police themselves were. They kept asking the same questions, but it wasn't going anywhere. So Rosie and I... Well, we started to look into your kidnapping ourselves."

"Jay." I don't know where this is going, but the anticipation is not helping the tremor starting in my hands. Of course he notices and reaches to lace our fingers together.

"Let me get this out?" He's almost pleading with me. "Rosie's good at making friends. Always has been."

I hum in agreement.

"Well, it turns out she's good at making friends in all sorts of high and low places. She has a talent for navigating dark corners."

"What on earth does that mean?" She pauses. "Like, mercenaries like Cy and Ember?"

I figured out their "occupation" pretty early into my stay. The extensive personal armory is a pretty big giveaway. Jay slumps a little at my words.

"Yeah. Like Cy and Ember, but all different sorts."

"You're making me nervous. Where is this going?"

Hesitation is never a good thing, but every time Jay does, it's like all the oxygen is stolen from the room until he voices the next part of his story. Time passes in silence before everything comes pouring out of him.

"I was angry and impatient. The police weren't doing shit. Like, they hadn't even found the guy who took you." He drops his head to rest against mine. "They called at one point to see if I recognized a name. We ran with it." His breath is hasty, and I can hear his heartbeat speeding up from where my ear rests against his neck.

"We found the guy and took him to this barn. Or really, someone Rosie found did. The coward spilled everything. He told us about taking you and where he took you. Told us about who you were with and what they wanted with you." He took a breath before continuing. "There was so much blood. And his screams. Goddess, the way he begged me to stop. But I didn't. I needed the violence, I think. I'm sorry." He buries his face in my hair.

The pain in his words shakes me. It's the first time I've ever heard true regret come from Jay, but it isn't for what he did, it's more like the fact he told me. Like he regrets telling me because he thinks it will change how I see him.

"You tortured him."

"I killed him." He looks me dead on. It's the first time he looks at me since beginning his confession. "And I don't regret it."

Whatever shame he felt while telling his story is replaced with a confident rage.

It's sexy.

"I needed the violence. I still do sometimes. Since then, Rosie's asked me to help out a couple of her new friends. Turns out I'm pretty good at it."

"You killed a man."

He nods. "A couple, but he was the first."

"For me."

Another nod.

I contemplate what he's told me. But I can't find fault with him. I can easily picture Jay with a gun or a knife in hand. The exhaustion I saw in him yesterday makes sense when he described what he endured himself. The fact that he did it for me, because of me?

We've both been through hell, and he came back the Reaper.

I turn to face him and kiss him. Hard.

Gods, I love this man.

YOU

Jay

When she pulls back from the kiss, there is a fire in her eyes.

"Is it wrong that I'm getting turned on right now?" she asks.

To say I'm shocked by her words is an understatement. I don't expect my confession of torturing and murdering a man to get this kind of response. If anything, I thought she would be appalled.

Fear ate at me for weeks. Fear I would tell her what I'd done, and she would see me as a monster. Every day we were separated, I thought about her reaction.

"What, from the torture and murder?" I laugh tentatively.

"No. Well, yeah, kinda." She rearranges herself on the bed so she's tucked tighter against me, but now she can see me fully.

I don't really have an answer for her. So instead, I shrug.

"Legality aside, did it help?" she asks while reaching for my hand again.

I don't have to think about it for a single moment.

"It's how we found out where you were," I confess. "Rosie's become a broker of sorts. She's good at it too. We hired the mercenaries through a third party after that. Paid them their fee, and now you're here. It's all I wanted. I wanted you back, and the details didn't matter."

I'm tracing my fingers across her arm with my free hand. It feels good to touch her. To have her in my arms. To breathe her in.

I'll lose myself in this woman forever if she lets me.

Burying my face in her hair, I voice the fear tormenting me. "Do you think it makes me a monster?"

"No. I don't think it does, Jay. The world isn't quite so black and white as I used to think." She bites down on her bottom lip, and the blush rising on her cheeks makes me long to kiss her again. "It's kind of like one of those 'touch her and you die' things. Which is pretty sexy."

"Of course you would find some connection to all those books you read." My Cheshire grin makes her giggle.

"What can I say?" she mocks. "I'm a sucker for a good romance."

"And what, this is one of those stories?"

The weight of the moment shifts as we both remember our kiss from only moments before. It feels so easy between us. Shifting from confessions to intimacy to jokes.

"It can be," she says.

The emotions flashing through her expression are a mix of longing and sadness. There's hope there too. I lean in closer to her to draw out the hope.

"Does it make me the hero here? You're my damsel in distress?" I realize my mistake immediately when she tenses in my hold, the strain evident in her jaw. "No, not that. You'd be the badass who takes over the world," I correct.

The relief washing over her is a salve to some wound festering in me. I see it wash over her before she responds, and it soothes me to see her relax.

"Yeah, I think I could be. Or..." Seeing her worry her lip makes me ache for her in a carnal way, but I know it's her way of processing. I can't get distracted. This is about her. "What if the devil whispers in my ear and I become the bad guy? What if I end up the villain of the story?"

Not knowing where she is coming from makes my heart ache. I mean... what on earth would make my perfect girl think she's the villain?

"I think if there's one thing we learned from our four years in school, it's that villains are rarely what they appear to be. Underneath it all, they're as human as the rest of us," I say.

"It feels cold. The anger, I mean. Not raging like everyone says it's supposed to," she says.

The change in her demeanor mirrors the change in topic. She's scared.

"I promise you it won't feel this way forever." I'll make sure of it.

"It feels like... It's like I'm alive, but I'm not living anymore. I don't know how to." She curls tighter into me. "Jay, I don't know what hope looks like anymore. I can't." Her breath is ragged.

"Then I'll be right next to you while you look for it. I'm never gonna let you do anything alone ever again. You're not even allowed to take a shit without me, okay?"

Even though I can't see it, I feel her smile.

"Jay?"

"Yeah?"

"How do you think this all ends?"

I cling to the hope she isn't talking about anything immediate, but the subtext is still there.

"What kind of ending do you want?"

But it's her turn to grin like an idiot when she responds. "A happily ever after, of course."

"Then that's what you'll get. I'll make sure of it, baby doll."

Without thinking, I kiss the point where her neck meets her jaw. Her breaths turn shallow, and when she turns to look at me, we drink each other in.

"You haven't called me that in a long time."

"What? Baby doll?"

"Yeah. Not since that night, after we met on Halloween."

I must look like a smug asshole. "You're forgetting about another very important night though."

The sudden blush rising in her cheeks flushes through her body quickly. My wandering hands stray from the safety of her arms to the soft skin poking out from beneath the T-shirt she wears. My lips trail to her collarbone, where I tease her through the worn fabric.

Then bite, hard.

She gasps and arches into me.

"You were a very good doll for me that night. The perfect plaything." I breathe the words into her ear. "I told you something then. Do you remember it?"

She goes still. Her sharp intake of breath tells me she definitely remembers.

"It was years ago... You never..." The words fall out of her rapidly with no thought fully completing itself. "We never... I thought..."

"I know." I debate not telling her my most vulnerable truth. But this is Julia, my best friend, my other half; there's no holding back between us. "I made you a promise, but it's never been about that for me. I want you. I didn't realize it until you were taken. But I want you. I want everything with you."

Everything stills, and I pray to whoever is listening I didn't push her away.

"Then take me," she says. Satisfaction swells in my chest. Quickly followed by an intense lust. "Please."

Her chest rises and falls more rapidly with each breath, and the movement draws my eyes to the peaks of her taut nipples. I smirk, remembering how she liked it with me last time. How she embraced everything I gave her. Rough or gentle, it didn't really matter. How she'd gone past her point of comfort with me to find a new kind of paradise amidst the pleasure and pain.

"You want me to take you? Then you give me everything. Every moment of fear, doubt, pain, and pleasure. You give them all up to me."

My hand reaches up to brush her nipple lightly before circling endlessly.

"Yes," she gasps.

"The man. The one I killed?" I pause, looking for acknowledgment. "Do you want to know what I did to him?"

I take her nipple between my fingers and slowly twist until she whines out a yes, making my own core throb in anticipation. I can sense her hesitation, but she's overwhelmed by the sensation of me stroking her body.

"I pulled out his teeth one by one," I murmur into her ear. "I watched him gag on his own blood. I cut out his tongue and watched him die slowly."

My hands move down her body to caress all of her curves as my recounting spills from my lips. I take my time to explore every bend in her body. Over her shirt my fingers explore the swell of her breast, the curve of her stomach, and journey towards where I crave to touch her.

By the way she squirms in my hold, I can tell this is turning her on. She wants this. She wants me. She wants my violence and my anger, but also my adoration.

"I wanted him to suffer as much as I did. I wanted him to feel as desperate for air as I did. Because I couldn't breathe after he took you."

My teeth scrape along the tender spot where her neck meets her collarbone.

"Jay," she pleads.

My lips journey up her neck to her ear, where I nip gently. My hands continue to play with her.

"All I ever want is to take care of you. I would give everything for you. Do anything for you. Not because you can't, but because I can."

The way my hands lightly trail along her body allows me to feel every movement she makes. She's nearly shaking in my arms. Her body wants and craves me.

"I always need you, but I've never been sure you need me. And suddenly, you did. You know what I thought about as his blood drained from his body?" At the mention of my violent desires, her hips rock up, begging for my touch.

I can't help but place kisses along her neck and hair. I need to touch her, feel her. I need the reminder she's here in my arms. And I am never letting her go.

"How good you would look with his blood on your lips. How beautiful you would be covered in the crimson evidence of his suffering. Every scream he uttered, every time he gagged while desperately trying to breathe, I imagined you were beside me. I wished I could walk up to you as we waited for him to die and kiss you breathless."

I do just that.

The kiss is frightful and urgent. Our tongues twist with each other, seeking the connection we so missed. Our passion is desperate and destructive. As we kiss, she squirms, and when I come up for air, I can see her rubbing her thighs together, seeking the friction she craves.

Reaching under her, I grasp her by the thighs and lift her. Her knees pull apart, and her feet land softly outside of my own.

Though still fully clothed, she is on complete display for me.

"Do you like this, baby doll? Do you like when I handle you like my plaything? When I tell you all of my dark and depraved secrets?"

The way she responds to my fingers lightly trailing up and down her body gives me my answer.

I shift her so her back is flush with my chest. I stroke lightly against her inner thighs, slowly caressing firmly enough to feel beneath the fabric of her sweatpants. She is still fully dressed, yet her body responds as though it were her delicate skin under my fingertips.

I love teasing her like this. Feeling how restless and desperate I make her. Touching her makes her impassioned. My hands trace every part of her body. My lips kiss every inch of skin they can reach. I spend my time rediscovering every inch of her.

But part of the fun is holding her off. Every time she tenses up, I stop right on the edge. Whenever she begins to beg, I slow down even further. She tries to draw her legs back together, but I am right there to pull them apart and forcefully keep them open.

I want her to unravel for me. Not for what any set of hands can do for her, but for me.

Me.

The mirror on the dresser gives me a perfect view of everything. Her eyes are shut, and she is arching back with her head leaned back over my shoulder. Everything in her body is taut and tense, waiting for a release that won't come easily.

"Do you need to come, baby doll?"

Her first tear makes me ask, and her response doesn't disappoint.

"YES! Fuck. Please!" Each word is separated with a panting breath. "I need to come. Please, Jay. I need you to touch me."

"Oh, but I have been." I chuckle.

"You know what I fucking mean." Her frustration only fuels my desire for her.

This is when she is most beautiful. When she fights. It's when she's alive.

Her impatience is endearing though, and I decide to be merciful.

"You're allowed to come as many times as you want. But do you remember what I want?" My fingers trail closer to her center as I speak. "Say it."

All she can do is whimper in response, but it's not enough.

"Do it. Count for me, baby." My command is as sharp as my smack on her pussy. At the impact, she cries out and falls apart in my arms.

"One." She chokes on the word.

I can feel the shock waves of pleasure rolling through her body. My hands grip her by the thighs to keep her spread wide open as she rides out her orgasm, denying her body the respite it tries to find by curling up. Her entire body shakes with violent tremors, but I don't let go. When she starts to twist, trying to escape my hold, I bring my arm around to secure her by the waist and throw my leg over her own. When her whines and whimpers turn into cries, I can tell she has reached the peak. She's going to fall hard and fast. And I'll be right there to catch her.

"So good for me," I praise as my lips trail her jawline.

Trapped in my arms, she struggles against my hold, but as her crashing tide withdraws, she begins to settle against me.

My free hand goes to her pussy, and my fingers tap against her core at a frantic pace. I want to hear her crying for release and hear her scream my name.

When her hips began to rock up into my touch, I switch the pacing and began to rub my hand up and down her center, still covered by her clothes. Each time she tries to push me away, I hold her pussy firmly to remind her who it belongs to.

Her shrieks transform into a burst of desperate laughter.

"So needy," I tease while nipping at her collar.

This time when she squirms, I don't stop her. I let her make every attempt to get away from me. I let her have the illusion she can take her pleasure from me.

But it isn't her decision to make.

In her attempt to escape my persistent touch, she falls to the side, so she lies in my lap, on display for me to play with. My hands graze her sides from her hip up to her collarbone. I reach for her wrists and take them in one hand to hold above her head while my other uses a single finger to trace the column of her neck and tilt her face to me.

"Do you know why I have you count how many times you come?" I ask, giving her a moment to catch her breath. "Because every number you breathe only tells me you want more. Because you need to know how much of you belongs to me."

My hand reaches for her center and slides beneath the waistband of her pants. I find her bare under them, and I redouble my efforts. The increasing pressure makes her buck and moan under my touch. Moans turn into whimpers and whimpers into desperate pleas.

"Again. Come for me, baby."

With a gasp, desperate for air, I feel her break. Her body shakes with tremors and twitches as she rides the wave of pleasure.

I release her hands and let her turn into herself. I only give her a minute before reaching for her, but I pause when I register her silence.

"Tell me to stop, and I will." But gods, I hope she won't.

"Please. Don't. Stop."

XXIII

SEX & STARDUST

Juliana

My words come out on breathless whimpers, but when I feel Jay shifting beneath me to retreat, I panic. My hand snaps to grab him by the wrist and keep him in place. My head tilts slightly to turn and meet his gaze while I lie limply in his lap. All I see is hesitancy.

He thinks I want him to stop? Fuck no.

There isn't enough air in my lungs, and my thoughts are too scrambled to get out real words.

"Two," I force.

I feel him shift out from underneath me before his weight settles on top of me and his lips crash into my own. The single word seems to erase whatever hesitancy I saw in his eyes because all that remains is a flame, like an out of control bonfire. I know Jay is a passionate partner, but how he touches me sets off every nerve in my body. Everything is so sensitive, yet all of me is screaming for more.

"You stop counting, I stop. Say red, I stop. Got it?" he says.

"Yes, sir." And if that doesn't drive the flames higher. "Green. Twelve. I don't care. More." With any other person, the whine in my voice would be humiliating, but with Jay, it simply is. There is no judgment between us, so I relax into our roles.

"What I'm hearing is you want to know what it's like to be drenched on my fingers. You want me to feast on your pussy and scream my name while you come. Am I right, baby doll?"

Gods, I want that so badly. I love how he can't keep his hands off of me. How his touch seems to cherish every inch of me. The same flame in his eyes rumbles in his voice when he talks to me like this. But it's the way he caresses me that feels nothing short of paradise.

He waits for an answer, but I don't know what to give him. I want everything.

"All of it. Everything. Please, sir."

"I love it when you use that name for me. The way you plead for me." He's standing to the side of the bed, and his hands make their way to the waistband of my pants. "I'm going to make you beg for me. Then you'll beg for mercy."

Darkness lingers in his words, and it's sexy as hell.

How have I never had this before with him? There was once, years ago, but it was nothing like this. I don't have time to think because his thumbs dip under the band and drag the sweatpants down.

Other than the few items Ash got for me, I'd been lucky to be able to mostly borrow clothes while I'd been here. They aren't anything special, but Jay makes the worn-out extras feel like the most drool-worthy lingerie.

I lift my hips slightly as he pulls them down before climbing back onto the bed. When he leans me forward and reaches for the hem of my shirt again, I hesitate. Without thinking, I try and move his hands away.

"What?" His concern at my response changes something in him. This isn't my sexy "sir". This is my best friend, Jay. The man who worries about me endlessly and whose face displays only concern.

"It's just..." I feel unsure. Hesitant. I hate it. "I have scars."

He props me up on my forearms and reaches to pull his own shirt off over his head.

"So what? I have scars too," he says.

Looking at him bare before me, I marvel at his figure. I reach out to run my fingers over the faint lines on his chest.

"Yeah, but you chose those. I..." I fiddle with the edge of my shirt. I already miss the pure lust of only moments ago. "I didn't."

"Look at me." He moves me so we're fully facing

each other. Our bodies closely press together as he holds himself above me. "I didn't choose my scars any more than you did. They came about differently, but I didn't choose them." I instinctively try to look away and break eye contact, but he reaches and pulls my attention directly to his gaze.

He searches my face for a moment.

"Scars tell a part of our story. Nothing more. There's nothing to be ashamed of."

My hands trace over the faint lines upon his chest, his own story lines. My gaze wanders his body while I chew on his words. My thoughts drift along with it.

"I know that look, and whatever you may be thinking, you're wrong." I look up at the forceful snap in his tone. "I once counted and kissed every stretch mark on your body. When we first opened the club, I dragged you to the hospital because you stopped eating. I held you every time you came home from a date with another fatphobic asshole. Do you really think a few new scars are going to change how I see you?"

"It's not a few, Jay." I know my sudden anger is a defense mechanism. A pathetic attempt to keep him away from me, but of course he knows exactly how to bring it down.

Take over. Please, Jay.

As though he can hear my thoughts, he thrusts his hand up to dig his fingers in my hair and pulls my head back. The motion arches my body up and presses me tightly against him.

"Doesn't matter, baby. They're mine to count, treasure, whatever I want."

His lips let out a breath at my neck, and I shiver. The distraction allows him to draw the shirt up and over my head with his free hand.

Then I am bare. No bra. Nothing.

Just me.

Everything is exposed, and the sheer vulnerability of the moment threatens to douse out the flicker of lust from before.

He drops his hands and moves to get off the bed. For a moment, I think he'll leave me here like this. Instead, he stands to take off his shoes and socks, but he turns away from me before peeling off his tight jeans. He works them over his tight ass and down his legs until he stands there in nothing but his briefs.

This man definitely knows how to put on a show.

Returning to the bed, he makes his way between my knees. His callused hands trail up and down my exposed sensitive skin. They trail from my ankle up to my knee and continue to brush up to my center.

His touch is intoxicating, but the sight of him kneeling on the bed between my legs is a power trip in and of itself. He leans down to place kisses along my inner thigh, and my breath catches when he stops right before reaching where I need him. I can feel his breath on me, and I can't suppress the whine attempting to leave me.

"Do you need something, doll?"

I could kill him for making me wait. The glimmer of mirth in his expression says he enjoys teasing me like this. He shifts back onto his heels as he looks at me and traces my body with his gaze. I need the warmth of his touch on my body. The sensation of his touches fades too quickly, and I'm an addict craving more.

He pulls down his hair from its messy bun.

"You're going to want to hold on for this."

Never call the man a liar.

Jay's singular focus is a previously unknown high. He follows through on every promise. His fingers expertly stroke me to draw out orgasm after orgasm. His tongue moves in patterns while his hands trace their mirror image on my tits.

I lose count at nine.

Every fiber of my being is on fire. It all feels so good. Yet every sensation against my skin is too much. The scratch of the bedding and the light breeze from the AC make me want to claw my eyes out. The washcloth he uses to clean me up is my nemesis.

I don't remember when the tears begin, but when he reaches for the blanket at the end of the bed, another involuntary sob breaks out of me.

"Baby doll. Shhh…"

Only his touch seems soothing. His fingers push back the hair from my face, and he traces my features with his fingertips. Everything else hurts, but his touch is the balm I need.

He tries to wrap me in the blanket. But he presses his front against my own this time, and it seems to dull some of the sensations.

I feel his hands running up and down my body underneath the harsh fabric. A sigh escapes every time his hands change direction, and I feel the light scrape of his short nails against my skin before the sensation of his fingertips returns.

It's the delicate kiss he places on my forehead that breaks me. A full round of sobs begins. These are different though. This is the emotional collapse I've been dreading for months.

Sobs break out of me, but Jay doesn't flinch at all. He pulls me in closer to him and holds me while I cry.

"I'm sorry. I'm so sorry," I say, bawling.

His arms tightly band around me, and his hands hold me so my face presses into the crook of his neck. I breathe in his scent of sweat and something smelling like Halloween, like pumpkin spice and pine. With each breath I take, my heart rate starts to steady, and my sobs begin to break up.

After a while, I drift off to sleep in his arms.

I'm broken beyond repair and yet finally whole with him.

I wake up to the sun setting in the west-facing windows of the bedroom. Jay stands to the side of the bed unpacking the bags he brought with him, dressed only in the dark jeans he wore earlier.

His body moves in such a way that draws my eye to every flex and bend of his muscles. My eyes follow his shoulders down to his strong hands, which delicately fold my clothes before placing them in drawers. Sleep still in my eyes, I let them trail over his torso when they catch on a dark pattern on his skin where his jeans hang loose, inches above the dip at his hip. I sit up and lean to run my fingers along the small space where the black ink peaks out.

"When did you get this?"

He stops his task and turns to sit down on the edge of the bed.

"After you were…" The silent understanding hangs between us. "I needed to feel something and thought a tattoo might do it."

"Can I see it?"

Pulling down the edge of his jeans as he stands, he reveals a beautiful pair of wings surrounded by words in script.

"Jay." I let out a gasp in shock.

Intertwined with the shading around the wings is a phrase: Let nothing stand in your way.

I thought I was all cried out, but I choke on the words from the first show we did together: *Angels in America*.

"Yeah," he says.

Jay lowers himself next to me on the bed, and we both sit there in silence together for a while as the words hang between us.

"You got it for me, didn't you?"

"I mean, I got it for me, but yeah, I needed something of you then, and it felt right."

I can't help but tear up at his words.

"Baby, no. Please, no more tears." I lean into his touch when I feel his hands on my face, wiping away my tears.

"I like when you call me that. Baby. Never babe. Always baby or baby doll," I say with a shaky breath.

"Or doll, when I'm feeling especially Guys-and-Dolls-esque." He chuckles.

"Yeah, you want to see me in one of those gingham chickadee dresses." I giggle.

Goddess. When was the last time I giggled?

"Damn right I do." He places a soft kiss on my nose. "You'd look hot as fuck in the skimpy little outfit. Legs for days, and I'd be drooling, dreaming of your ass under a short little petticoat." As he speaks, he reaches out to grab me by my plump ass and brings me to straddle him. My hands go to rest on his chest, and I aimlessly trace his collarbone.

"You wanna tell me about what happened?" The words are so hesitant. He's walking on eggshells.

"Yes…"

"Yes, but…"

"I wanna tell you. I do. But, b-but…" I take a deep breath before continuing. "I don't remember a lot."

He contemplates for a while before responding. "Makes sense. Your brain is trying to protect you from the memories. That's normal."

"I remember feeling a void sometimes. Then there were times when I thought I was at camp. Riding horses, swimming, or dancing. But there are flashes of some things."

Patience is neither of our virtues, but I appreciate Jay's willingness to sit with me and listen.

"And I remember after," I say.

"Tell me about it?" He asks gently.

"I woke up in a bed," I start slowly. "I wasn't tied up. So I knew I'd been moved."

My hand reaches to cup Jay's jaw when he clenches

it at my retelling. I can tell I need to rush through this story. Otherwise, something is going to break. Either he would break something, or I would break down.

"There was a guy, and he brought me to his room there. And he took care of me. Tried to clean me up and feed me." I laugh at the memory. "He was kinda cute."

Jay's eyebrow rises. How does he do that with one eyebrow?

"He was physically cute. Well... hot, really. And he was kind. He offered me something to eat, but I told him I was allergic, and he went into this kind of frenzy. It was sweet. I don't know why, but he wanted to help me. He left to talk with someone at some point, and for that week I mostly slept. But he was kind, and I felt safe with him. I know it makes no sense, but I did. I do."

I blush at the memory of Griffin's hands on me. How his lips and tongue did magical things to my body. How he made me forget for a while and distracted me from pain.

"I kind of slept with him. Well... he went down on me."

There is no judgment on Jay's face. I feel the need to be honest with him, especially after what happened between us.

"You think maybe you were just coping?" I blush because he's right. He always is. "It's okay, Julia. You had a lot going on." His hands cup my face, and our foreheads meet to rest on one another. "If he helped you, then that's all I care about. If he hurt you, I'll kill the bastard."

Rocking back at his anger, I see him in a new light. How he must have felt over the past weeks. How he found a new drive because of it.

"No! Goddess, no. Nothing like that. He was nice. I trust him." I search for some way to explain. How do you explain to one soulmate that you found another? "He said he was a cop, right? I mean, all cops are bastards. But he wanted to help."

"Sounds like he did a lot more than help," Jay grumbles.

"Jay!" I slap him playfully.

"What? Can you blame me? From your description, some hot cop with a savior complex helps you out of a *kidnapping* situation." His head drops back then. "Gods. No. Not like that. I'm not judging you. It sounds like he kinda took advantage of you."

"No, Jay. Nothing like that. If anything, I took advantage of him."

"Riiight."

"Jay, seriously. Griffin is a good boy."

The bewildered look Jay gives me catches my attention.

"Did you say his name is Griffin?" he asks.

"Yeah…"

"Shit. This makes so much more sense." He runs his fingers through his dark hair and sighs before standing to pace the room. "The detective assigned to your case said they were pressured to close it because they didn't have the resources anymore. At that point, I already knew you were here, so I was fine with it. But the detective said there was another guy who was asking questions. The woman basically warned me about him."

Jay turns to face me, and the determination in his expression is clear.

"The guy reached out to me. I couldn't exactly appear to stop caring that you were missing even though I knew where you were, and I certainly wasn't going to tell this guy. We met up for coffee, but something was off about the whole thing. He seemed way too invested, and he called you Jules."

"Oh."

"His name was Griffin. I have his card somewhere with his number." Jay turns to search through his stuff strewn on the floor.

My heart is hammering in my chest. What if this is him?

"He promised to find me," I whisper.

"What?" Jay turns back to me.

"Griffin, when Cy and Ember took me away. He promised he would find me."

"Okay..."

"Jay, if this is the same, Griffin, I need... I d-don't know what I need. But what if it's him?"

"Then we call him."

Simple as that. Call him. Of course, Jay has the most logical solution.

"You care about him." It isn't a question. It's a statement of what Jay already knows.

"Yeah, I think I do. Is that okay?"

"Juliana..." Well, this is serious then if he's using my full name. "You're my best friend. I will be right by your side even if you don't want me there. You don't have to earn my friendship or affection, and it's *definitely* not going to disappear because you have feelings for someone else. This isn't a conditional thing. Never has been. Nothing's changed."

"I don't know what I did to deserve you." I reach forward as I kneel on the bed to wrap my body around his, putting my arms around his neck, and his hands come to rest on my back.

I feel him press a kiss into my hair. "Here's the thing. You did nothing, and that's the way it should be."

I love the way he holds me. It's like I'm something delicate, and yet I never doubt how strong I can be when I'm in his arms.

After several heartbeats, I back away.

"So..." I let my sentence go unsaid in hopes I won't have to voice it out loud.

"So?"

Drat.

"What do we do about Griffin?" I ask.

"Maybe let's talk to the others before we do anything else. Kay?"

I nod. I've been more settled since Jay arrived. Something new has emerged between us, and yet everything is the same. Somehow, despite everything, I feel like maybe there is a chance things will be okay.

TROUBLE

Cy

"**Y**ou fuckin' with me? You want to bring *who* inna this shit?" My voice booms around the living room. So much so that Kieran cowers with his hands over his ears on the couch. I grab the headset off the coffee table as I make my way over to him.

"Sorry, kid. Didn't mean to get so loud." Fiddling with the headphones, I extend my arm, presenting my offering to him. He looks up at me with those big eyes of his, and I smile. Grabbing the headphones, he races off with the dog at his heels.

There's defeat in the sigh I push out.

They're all idiots if they think we're doing this.

"Cy, consider for a moment..." I appreciate Ember trying to get me to calm down, but they're really not helping. My frustration is justified, and I'm not ready to let it go yet.

"No, we're not considering shit, Ember."

We all gathered in the living room after the two lovers finally emerge from the girl's bedroom. Everyone's well aware of what went on in there. Kieran was even sequestered to Ember's workroom while the two worked whatever the fuck they needed to get out of their systems.

They both seem happier though, and I envy it a bit.

Not that they were happy, but that the guy is the reason. Hard as it is to admit, there is a part of me that's jealous. After the months she's lived under our roof, not once has she smiled the way she does when she looks at her friend. Lover?

Whatever the fuck it is, it's complicated. I don't do complicated.

"We already been through this with him," I growl, gesturing to her friend. "It's too much of a security risk bringing in more people. Not strangers and 'specially not *cops*."

I look over at the others, and the girl's expression nearly flattens me.

She's put up a damn strong front. Takes everything I throw at her and never complains. But she's been going through the motions. I see it every time I'm with her. She does what she's told, what she's pushed to do, and not of her own will. More like she seems directionless, and it's easier to follow than lead.

But she is a leader. She needs to find her fight.

The look she gives me holds the same brokenness from when she arrived. Gone is the content expression from earlier.

I look at Ember, hoping to clear the suffocating feeling building in my chest. No luck there. They're as wrapped around Juliana's finger as the rest of us.

Fuck.

The girl walks over and sits across from me. My gaze travels from the hand she's placed on my thigh up to meet her eyes.

"Cy." When she says my name like that? Fuck me. "You saw him. He cares about me. I don't think he's the bad guy here."

Remembering the look on the man's face from our rescue mission right before we left... yeah, the guy is smitten. She's probably right about that.

But a *cop*?

I don't know how to trust that. No matter how good of a guy he might seem. Doesn't even matter he probably saved us a lot of trouble getting her out.

Like a coward, I pull away and rise to escape the girl's gravitational pull.

"Sage, even you gotta see how bad of an idea this is," I say.

"I've met Griffin a couple of times. He works for my husband." She looks to Juliana, whose expression crumbles before us, then forces her attention back to me. "I never knew he was a cop. He's been loyal to Arrick."

Vindicated, I turn around to see Juliana withdrawing. My resolve crumbles as the whispers of doubt in the back of my mind come forward.

"It's been over two months since this all started. Nothing's happened since. It will be fine. Look, if you're worried, then you go with Jay. Oversee everything," Ember says, caving.

"Not worried. Just think y'all bein' stupid." Jay chuckles at that, but I ignore him. "Fine. But I'm in charge. Every step of the way. Got it?"

"Yes, sir!" He salutes mockingly. I don't miss the wink he directs at Juliana though.

"So we're doing this?" The girl's words are timid but clear.

"Guess so, ti dife."

Ember gives me a knowing look, but I ignore them.

"Tèt zozo, call the guy. We leave in thirty," I say.

"Is that me?" Jay asks. "What does that even mean?"

"Dick head." Ember laughs.

"Well, that's oddly affirming." The guy chuckles.

I leave the room, shaking my head. Seems I can't even be a proper asshole to the guy.

Halfway down the hall on my way to the gym, I feel a hand clasp my own, and I spin to confront the person before relaxing when I realize it's Juliana.

"Thank you." Our hands still connected, she gives me a squeeze, which travels straight to my chest.

"Not doin' this outta the kindness of my heart, ti dife. Just know you'd be a brat about it if we didn't."

"Yeah, but I'd be your brat." Taking a step towards me, I realize how tall she is. She's formidable. A warrior if I've ever seen one. Her curves are in all the right places. I resist the urge to touch her, let my hands wander. And she's *flirting* with me. No mistaking that.

I shouldn't want her.

"Gotta grab my stuff." I release her hand and turn.

"Yeah, of course."

Thirty minutes later, Jay and I are in the SUV on our way to Bliss. The cop was summoned, and based on Jay's side of the conversation, the guy is more than eager to talk.

It's the middle of the day, but there's already a car parked in the lot when we arrive at the club. The guy leaning against it immediately pushes off and moves towards us. Car parked, we both get out, and Jay walks over to meet the guy.

"Let's go inside."

He nods, but his energy is off... for a cop. He's like a puppy dog. It's kinda cute. Big formidable cop with tattoos covering every visible inch of his body, and he's practically bouncing with energy.

Barely two steps into the club, he jumps straight in.

"So you wanted to see me. Is it about Jules? Is she okay?"

Oh, it's Jules, is it?

Jay looks to me for direction, but I shrug. He's on his own here. This wasn't my idea.

"Why don't we go to her office," Jay says. I'm going to snap the guy's wrist if he keeps stalling.

Safely in the office, Jay starts up. "You need to come clean, Griffin. Why are you so invested in this? You're not even assigned to her case. The case is fucking closed."

The guy, Griffin, glances over at me. He's still unaware that Jay already knows. His hand reaches up to run through his dark hair. A nervous habit, probably. Benefit of not doing introductions is I'm still an unknown, and unknowns are threatening. I can clearly tell I'm having the desired effect on this kid. Sure, we'd met the one time, but it seems like he's purposefully avoiding my gaze.

"We can't trust you if you don't fill us in," Jay continues.

You can see the debate going on in the kid's mind.

How in the hell is he an undercover cop?

We're all standing around, but the kid slumps into

a chair when he seems to make up his mind and relent.

"I met her, Jules. Um... I-I am technically on assignment. Arrick has me on an errand looking for his wife and kid again. A-and her."

Shit. He's talking about the doctor and her kid.

He turns to look at me then. "Look, if you're here, then you've gotta know where she is."

He looks back and forth between Jay and me.

"Please, I wanna make sure she's okay." The sincerity in his voice is clearly working on Jay, but I'm not quite so trusting.

"You're a cop," I say. He flinches. "And you handed her over."

"Yeah. So what? You were her best chance of getting out of there alive. I couldn't do anything without more time."

The fight comes back into him, and I grin at the change. Maybe this pup possesses a bit more bite than it seems.

"You wanna tell him?" I direct this to Jay.

I can tell he is still debating internally, but I know he'll end up doing what Juliana asked. After all, it's *her* asking.

"She's safe." The audible sigh of relief from the kid is humorous. "And she's asking for you."

"What, really? Can I see her?" He stops suddenly and furrows his brow, suspicion taking over. "Wait...

why are you making this so easy?"

"Well, Juliana is asking. Plus, Sage vouched for you," I say.

"Sage? Sage Mathieson?" His shock seems completely genuine. "Shit, probably not good I know. Shit."

"Look. You wanna see her or what?" I cut in.

"Yeah. Of course! It's just complicated if Sage is involved. That's all."

"Course it is," I mumble. "Ain't none of this been easy from the start."

Like before, we make arrangements for meeting, and then Griffin departs, leaving only Jay and me in the club.

It's already decided Jay will stay behind and continue his normal routines, much as it seems to pain both him and Juliana to be separated. But it needs to appear like nothing is out of the ordinary, and having him up and disappear is not a good way to do things.

The parking lot is empty when Jay and I exit the club. Plan is to drop him off at his apartment before going back home.

Pulling out of the lot, everything appears normal, but something has the hair on the back of my neck standing up. I'm on alert, and something feels wrong. My head on a swivel, I keep an eye out as I drive, following Jay's directions.

Slowly, I pull over to the curb in front of his building. Then I spot a car I thought I'd seen before.

"Jay. Don't look back. There's a car following us."

When he starts to move, I reach over to slam him back into the seat.

"I said. Don't. Look."

"What should we do?" His voice is level and firm. I'm impressed at the lack of fear I would expect from someone new to this world.

"We redirect and lose them."

It takes an hour of driving aimlessly around the city before I am confident we lose the tail. I'm a bit turned around. It takes time for Jay to guide us back to his home. We arrive, and Jay begins to climb out, but I grab his arm.

"Don't fuck this up because you're too eager. There's a new normal. Accept it. Or else you're gonna get hit with some hard truths." My gaze meets his own cool jade-green eyes. He doesn't fight me, but he doesn't crumble under my attention either. I can appreciate that about the guy.

He doesn't understand, but I hope my words sink in eventually. If he cares about her safety, it's not me who needs to be on alert.

The drive home is quiet, but my thoughts keep circling back to the car from earlier. Ember and I have lived under the radar for too long for someone to randomly take such interest in our activities. The girl, on the other hand, everyone seems to be invested in.

Not that I blame them.

THE DEVIL IS A GENTLEMAN

After Juliana's friend and Cy head out, she retreats, leaving a heavy weight in my stomach. *You couldn't have known.*

Well, I know pieces. I know she was hurt, that Cy and Ember rescued her from Mathieson Enterprises, that Arrick is not the man I knew him to be. But I refused to put the pieces together. I didn't want to face reality. I was putting it off.

My husband, Arrick, is not a good person. He was sweet at one point, but his anger was out of control right before Kieran and I left. He complained for months about how business was suffering. The paranoia consuming him was disturbing. But he never came back from the paranoia, and I lost the sweet man he was.

I figured it would blow over. His rants about how someone was stealing merchandise from him would dissipate.

How wrong I was.

The devastation on Juliana's face when I confessed my connection to the man who tortured her was heartbreaking.

On the other hand, the hope I saw in her eyes at the prospect of seeing Griffin makes me think she's clinging to something about her experience with him. I was not lying when I said he is loyal. I've only ever known the man as the gruff and socially withdrawn head of Arrick's security. His level of dedication to my husband was admirable. Well, until I realized the full scope of the business. Learning Griffin is one of the good guys? It's a small relief that makes all the difference.

Kieran even likes the man; he says Griffin makes the best cookies. Witnessing such a large man who handles a gun like it's an extension of his own body offering your nine-year-old a chocolate chip cookie is quite a sight. Perhaps I judged him too harshly. Kieran isn't one to take well to others, and the fact he trusts this man lends him some credibility in my mind.

When Juliana and Jay asked to bring Griffin here, I was hesitant. But I need answers, and maybe Griffin can finally provide some for me. Maybe he can help pull me out of this perpetual stillness I have lived in for almost four months. Maybe he's the thing that Juliana needs to pull her from wherever she went moments ago.

Watching how Juliana shut down when I mentioned Arrick had me digging my nails into my palm in an attempt to maintain some level of composure. I can only imagine what she must have thought. Of what she's been through and what she thinks of me because of the connection.

I hope I haven't wrecked the friendship we have developed over the past weeks.

I find myself hesitating outside of her doorway.

This has to happen sometime.

I knock and wait for her answer with my heart thundering in my chest.

When she opens the door, my breath catches. Her eyes shine with tears, and her skin is red and blotchy. She's a mess. Rightfully so.

Part of me hates how beautiful she looks with tear tracks running down her face. She's vulnerable, and I'm basking in being able to see this side of her.

"Can I come in?" I ask, hoping she doesn't turn me away. I would understand if she does.

Opening the door wider, she lets me in, and my heart rate begins to slow from its nervous patter.

I need to start this conversation, but for once, I don't know how. I should be used to giving bad news. I worked in an ER for over a decade. This shouldn't be so hard.

But with her, it feels impossible.

"I imagine you are feeling caught off-guard," I watch

her as she physically she turns into herself. "I should have told you sooner, but I didn't want… well, it doesn't matter. I should have told you."

"Thank you."

Her simple answer brings back the nervous energy that was starting to dissipate from my body.

"Can we sit?" I ask.

She nods, and we move over towards the bed, where she pulls the blanket around herself in a cocoon.

"Arrick… we met in college. I was nineteen, and he was charming. I fell for him hard and fast." I look to her for any sign she doesn't want to hear this. Her hands are tightly clutching the blanket around her, and she won't meet my gaze, but there's nothing telling me she wants me to stop. "We were married for thirteen years before I had Kieran. I wanted to wait until I was done with med school and residency. I wanted to be settled into my career before having kids."

"Kieran's a good one." A small smile creeps onto her lips.

"Yeah, he is, isn't he? He likes you too, you know." I sigh, not knowing where I should go next with my story. "What do you want to know, darling? I promise to tell you whatever you want, but I don't want to hurt you."

She contemplates my words, and I'm grateful for the time together. I can only rely on the trust we've already built between us.

"It hurts that I didn't know." She starts to choke up, and I can tell she's holding back tears. "I don't understand."

"Understand what, darling?"

"I don't... I don't know. It hurts. I don't understand what I did to deserve what he did to me. And it feels like you're part of it somehow. I know it's not logical, but it hurts."

Reaching out to place my hand on her knee, I wish I could take some of the pain away from her.

"I didn't do anything wrong," she says, and her whole body shakes. "I've done everything right. I did everything right. I didn't do anything wrong."

"I know, darling. I'm so sorry this happened." She tries to bury the guilt, but by the way she holds herself it's still plainly evident. I move closer and reach to bring her into my arms. "None of this is your fault. Arrick isn't a good person. It's not your fault."

My reassurances bounce off of her. I feel so helpless. Normally, I can do something. There's something to fix. But, I can only sit with her, and it's making every hair on my body stand on end with tension.

She steels herself. "I need to know."

"Know what, darling?" My thumb rubs back and forth on her knee, hopefully offering her comfort.

"How he became a monster. Why he chose me."

This woman is incredible. Her resolve to push past her hurt, fear, and anger is inspiring. So I offer her the only truths I have.

"After college, I went to medical school. To support us, Arrick…" She flinches at his name. "He went to work for my family's distribution company. He worked his way up and eventually took over at a senior level. After my dad retired around nine years ago, right around the time Kieran was born, Arrick took over—moving the headquarters to Houston—and quickly built the company into what it is, Mathieson Enterprises. I never questioned how quickly it grew, but I should have."

She is finally looking at me, eager for every word.

"About three years ago, he started talking about how business was hurting. He was convinced someone was sabotaging the business and merchandise. He started to get angry, and eventually, his anger spilled into violence." I laugh at my own stupidity. "I see women in the ER all the time with telltale signs of DV, but in my own home, I didn't see it coming. The first time he hit me was in front of Kieran."

"Did he ever hurt him?" Her concern is endearing. How she's able to put her own hurt to the side for another.

"No, thank the Gods. But after, I kept as far away as possible."

"Good. Kieran doesn't deserve it."

"Neither do we, darling." I caress her face and look her dead in the eyes.

"How did you end up here?" she asks.

"With Cy and Ember?"

"Yeah."

"My husband isn't a good man, and like I said, he's distrustful. A little over a year ago, he took out a life insurance policy for Kieran and me. For ten million dollars."

Her jaw drops in shock.

"A few months ago, he had a fixer approach Cy and Ember with a bid. Said he needed a rival taken out. But you know them—they're mercenaries, but they have a certain moral code. They don't do families, no women or children. They took his money, well, the half given upfront, and hid us away instead."

"He tried to have you killed?" The words are spoken with breathy disbelief.

"I think he intended to have them stage it so he could get the life insurance money. That's why he hired them. He needed someone completely detached from him. But we disappeared instead." I brace myself for her reaction. "Honey, I think he singled you out because we left him. He needed someone to take his anger out on, and I think you remind him of me from when we were younger."

She takes it surprisingly well, and I continue. "I

didn't know about the illegal elements until Cy and Ember located you at the warehouse. Part of me didn't want to know. So I never pried."

"Compound."

"What?"

"Compound. Griff called it a compound."

"Okay, compound. I didn't know until they found you at the compound. And when they brought you back, I felt so guilty. I had a feeling he was at fault for what happened to you, but I couldn't bring myself to say anything."

Before she turns into herself, I grasp her gently by the chin and force her to look at me.

"Darling girl. This is not your fault. It's a chaos-of-the-universe thing, and I would do anything to take it away from you. You don't deserve this. But I'm right here if you need me."

Our foreheads rest together, and I deeply breathe in her honeysuckle scent.

"It doesn't matter if the trauma makes you stronger. You weren't supposed to be strong. You were supposed to be safe," I say.

I need her to understand she's safe with me. I would never hurt her. I would protect her as much as my own son.

I place a delicate kiss on her lips. A light brush between us. It's sweet and gentle, but there's heat there nonetheless.

She seems startled by the kiss, but with relief, I feel her body relax into me.

Lost in thought, I can see the gears in her head processing the patchwork of information I've given her.

"And Griffin?

"I don't know, but we can find out more when he gets here."

"But he's good, right?" There's a desperation in her voice. She needs to hear this from me.

"I hope so, honey. I really hope he's one of the good ones."

"Okay, thank you. I think I need to process." Her dismissal is clear, but I think she got what she needs. I hope she did.

"Kieran and I are here to stay, by the way. Ember set us up down the hall. I'm here for you if you need me."

I place another kiss on her forehead and move to leave.

"Sage?"

"Yes, darling?"

"No more secrets. Please, I can't handle anymore."

"Of course, honey."

My instinct is to go into the bathroom and wet a cloth to clean up her face. I want to bring her something to eat, make sure she drinks water, rub circles into her back until she falls asleep.

But she's asking to be alone. I hope she knows it's temporary.

She's not meant to be alone.

And she won't be anymore.

SIREN

Juliana

I guiltily avoid Sage for days.

It's not her fault she married the wrong person.

It's not her fault he's the cause of the worst experience in my life.

It's not her fault I'm broken.

It hurts that she didn't tell me. Thinking back though, I would have only handled it worse if she'd told me sooner. I am already falling apart, and I'm barely putting myself back together.

I need time to process. My entire body has been on high alert for forever, and while Cy has been teaching me physically how to fight, my first instinct is still flight.

When she came to my room, all I wanted to do was hide. I wanted to disappear. Hearing her truth in front of everyone made my heart stop, and in turn, all I wanted was for everything to freeze.

I'm so tired of surviving on momentum, of only making it to the next day because I made it through the last.

I'm alive but not living.

I'm floating through nothingness because I don't know if I want to go back to life.

Part of me is comfortable with the emptiness I've adjusted to. Part of me feels safe here.

Cy returned without Jay that day, and his absence makes me ache. I need him, and he isn't here.

Not that it's his fault. It's the plan. We're sticking to the plan.

The only bright spot is when I learn they met with Griffin and figured out a way for him to visit.

Similar to Jay's appearance, we arranged a pickup for him that would be outside of everyone's normal routines. He'll then go through the city on a circuitous path until Cy is certain it's safe to return home.

Home.

When did I start to think of this place as home?

I don't want to doubt Cy, but his caution seems over the top. When he got back from the meeting with Griffin, he swore up and down someone followed them for at least half an hour before he lost them. But at this point, why would someone still be trying to follow any of us? It's been over two months.

Nothing bad is going to happen.

The words are the mantra getting me through the day.

The day arrives before I know it, and Cy and Ember pick up a car from goddess knows where. The plates are surely stolen, and I know it's destined for a scrapyard immediately after this odyssey.

Today is the day.

Griffin is supposed to be here in an hour.

This is totally different from seeing Jay though. Reuniting with him is like coming home. There is comfort, safety, and security there.

With Griffin, there are butterflies in my stomach.

I'm *nervous*.

Which is ridiculous. I only know the man from a few days together.

Yes, his touch makes me melt, and the tender way he looks at me stops my heart, but I don't know him.

Not really.

But it's the first pleasant feeling since Jay left, and I'm grasping onto it desperately.

Ember calls to let us know they're on their way back, and Sage finds me pacing my room shortly after.

"Darling, you need to calm down."

I roll my eyes.

A woman really should know better than to tell someone to calm down.

She has a point though.

Why does this man twist me up like this?

What makes him so different?

And why don't I feel guilty about my feelings for him when I already have Jay?

I don't have time to question any of this though when I hear the garage doors open from downstairs.

I snap my head towards Sage and see how my panicked expression startles her.

In the moments I cannot avoid her, she walks around me on eggshells.

The nervous energy is turned back on me, transforming the butterflies in my stomach into hummingbirds.

I want to throw up.

Instead, I straighten myself. My dress hangs a little bit loose on my body, but thankfully it looks at least a little bit intentional. I run my hands down my sides and pray to whoever is listening that this doesn't blow up in our face.

I can feel Sage studying me, but she says nothing.

So I turn and march myself out of my bedroom.

Griffin's sitting on the couch and looks so out of place. In his hands, he has a box, and he's fiddling with the top nervously. The sight of this gorgeous, tattooed man with shining ocher eyes fiddling with anything is enough to make me melt.

He looks up, and we lock in on each other.

A warmth spreads through my body, and I want to run to him. We are only steps from each other, yet neither makes the first move. I gaze down at this man I momentarily thought to be a figment of my imagination.

Finally, he breaks the silence. "I... I made you these." Rising, he thrusts the box towards me.

A small smile escapes my lips, and I accept the gift gratefully from him. Looking inside, I see mini muffins of all things.

I can't help my laugh that breaks through.

"They're gluten-free." He blushes.

"They're perfect. Um... did you really make them?" I step towards him, and he visibly relaxes.

"Uh, yeah, I did." His hand reaches back to grip the hair at the base of his neck. The flex of his biceps grabs my attention, and I drool at the sight of his muscles flexing.

"Sage kind of spilled you're a stress baker." I giggle. There are other people in the room, but I don't care.

"Right. About that..." He steps towards me, but his eyes have traveled over to the woman in question. "I need to tell you some things."

My heart seizes.

No. I can't do this. I can't take any more bad news or heartbreaking truths.

I need something good.

He is supposed to be something good.

I take a step back from him, and Sage must sense

my distress because before I realize it, she's next to me, gripping me by the elbow.

"Griffin." She's welcoming, but it's forced. "Good to see you."

"Yeah, you too, Mrs. Mathieson."

"Please, Sage is fine. I really don't know how much longer I want to be a Mathieson." Sage's smile is thin, and I see the truth behind the words. There's so much anger and disgust. "Why don't we go somewhere more comfortable, okay? Maybe your room, Juliana?"

I nod in agreement and begin to follow her down the hallway with Griffin in front of me.

Before I even make it five steps, I feel a tug on my wrist. Turning, I see Ember looking at me with concern, Cy over their shoulder.

"You okay with him alone?" Ember asks.

Cy's look is brutal, but Ember is at least attempting to be understanding, or at least impartial.

"I won't be alone; Sage will be there."

Ember lets me go, but Cy's gaze keeps me in place.

"What?" I ask, exasperated. I'm so done with this man's shit.

His strong hand comes up to cup around the side of my neck. Not grasping, but lightly holding me in place. I can't help but lean into the touch. As much as I internally cringe at the automatic reaction, I can admit I crave the connection.

I keep expecting him to say something, and he almost starts to but changes his mind.

A brush of Cy's thumb across my jawline sends a shiver down my spine. Then he's walking away.

The man is a conundrum wrapped in an enigma.

I hurry to catch up with Sage and Griffin and reach them as they enter my room.

When I enter, Griffin is looking everywhere but at me. The calm, level-headed man I met weeks ago is nowhere to be found. Something is making him jumpy.

"Juliana, you should probably sit," Sage says and motions toward the bed, but I remain planted in place.

"No. I'm tired of people telling me to sit down just so I can get slapped in the face with more bad news."

There is a look passing between the two. Clearly, they spoke while I was with Ember and Cy. The concern in Sage's gaze shines brightly, and there are worry lines I want to smooth out on Griffin's face.

"Please, Jules," Griffin says.

I'm so tired of people pleading with me in that tone. Everyone thinks I'm going to fall apart at the slightest puff of air.

In fairness, a couple of weeks ago I would have and maybe I still will, but this is different.

I can hold my own. Can't I?

Finding it easier to concede than fight them on such a minor issue, I move to the bed and settle on the edge.

Looking to Griffin, I wait for the next blow.

"Arrick is looking for you." He turns to Sage. "Both of you."

For the first time, every memory comes flooding back.

All of them.

XXVII

SHE CALLS ME DADDY

Sage

Juliana sits frozen on the edge of the bed.

"It's more like he's hunting you. After you left, he sent me after you, Sage, and he wants you too, Jules. He's obsessing over you both," Griffin warns, going to kneel at Juliana's feet. "That's why I needed to see you. I needed to make sure you were somewhere safe."

Even when he takes hold of her hands, she remains unresponsive.

"Honey, what do you need?" I ask.

She needs to come back from wherever she retreated to. The emptiness in her eyes forces an unnatural terror through me.

"Darling, I need you here."

Something seemed to register with her when I call her darling. She starts to come back to herself, and I want to draw her out further.

I can't have her retreating to the same headspace I

found her in when we met. She has worked too hard to escape that place.

"Jules?" The man at her feet looks like he needs this woman to live. Something about his expression makes it clear he is completely besotted.

Having met Griffin multiple times over the years, it's surprising how easily he lays himself at her feet. He was so cool and collected in the past. Sure, he was warm and friendly with Kieran, but the man was all business other than those small moments.

His attentiveness shows clear adoration for the woman under my care. It seems their dynamic is different. He gives her something she needs.

"Do you like having him touch you?"

She is still quiet, but it is unsurprising. We've seen her cycle between various highs and lows during her stay with us. In the beginning, her fire raged, and passion drove her.

That is not the woman before me. I want the lively girl back. So much was stolen from her, and I don't want this for her. I want to see her strong and independent.

"What do you want from him, darling?"

She seems to study his face for a while, contemplating what she wants. But there doesn't seem to be a clear direction.

I'll give her the direction she needs. After Jay's visit,

we all know she's not touch averse. So I can focus here in the present.

"Do you want him to touch you?"

The heat flaring in her eyes is all the confirmation I need.

"Yes," she says.

"Undress and kneel again before her, Griffin."

I saw before how she reacts to people standing over her. The primal fear she expresses. Every time Cy trains with her, I worry he will pin her to the ground, and she will break. I want to avoid that at all costs.

Plus, this man looks stunning on his knees before her. He glares at me though. If not for Juliana's outright desire, I think he would walk away.

"My only interest is in her well-being. I am only asking on her behalf. Look at her. You heard her words. She wants this. So do you," I say.

He glances back to her for confirmation and then stands a couple steps back to undress.

I can see why she wants him. He shows a different light when he submits before her.

Once undressed, he settles back to his knees a few feet away from her. His cock thickening as he watches her.

"Crawl to her."

His muscles ripple and stretch as he lowers himself onto all fours. Prowling towards the darling girl before us. It's more attractive than I originally imagined. The man possesses a very appealing ass too. I can easily imagine spanking him while he pleasures her.

I know I want her, but I didn't expect to feel attraction to anyone else. Least of all him. He feels too close to Arrick. The reality of interacting with him is different though. He is nothing like Arrick, which calms the worries I originally conjured about him.

Watching Griffin is fascinating. His lust is palpable, yet he's pliable. He is here entirely for her. She is his sole focus. He is living completely in the moment. For her.

Juliana shifts, trying to find friction, pleasure. I can give that to her. *We* can give that to her. If she trusts us.

"Spread your legs for us, darling," I say.

Her eyes never leave Griffin, but she's questioning whether she wants to comply.

"Do you trust I have your best interest at heart?" I ask.

"Yes." The word is whispered, but there is no hesitation. She opens her legs to him.

"Go to her. Place your face right near her pussy. But don't touch. Just look," I tell Griffin.

His face is so close, and he is breathing deeply. Taking in her scent of arousal.

"Run your hands up her legs. Kiss and nip at her thighs. Brush your nose and lips across her, but nothing more."

His obedience is a weighty thing to hold in my control. I know it's all for her, but seeing him act out the fantasy building in my mind is erotic. I am growing hot and wet from the sight of them together.

Their connection is enthralling. How they feed off of each other. How they find balance. She needs to feel secure, as the panic attacks and nightmares she has been having aren't getting any better. He gives her that. The control, the power she needs.

I want her to find a sense of self. For her to release herself from the state of perpetual fear she seems to be stuck in. Maybe, just maybe, along with Griffin, we can give her that. Retrain her body to accept the comfort and support we all so readily offer.

There are many different responses to trauma, and right now, she is in a frozen state. Fight faded soon after Jay's return. I can tell she likes to escape everything by going to someplace deep within herself. It's a form of protection, but it isn't a long-term solution.

Looking at the two of them together, I know I can help her, but only if she is willing to help herself. Only she can save herself.

I stand apart from them as my plan finalizes in my mind. I move towards the pair while narrating every movement and decision.

"Darling, can you look at me?" I ask.

Her face turns to me.

"I want to do something for you. Will you let me?"

She contemplates the offer for an extended moment. The lack of change in her demeanor tells me she is ultimately comfortable, or at least open to the idea. Her short nod of approval is only confirmation of my expected outcome.

"I am going to come and sit behind you." I move slowly, giving her time to stop everything if she needs it. When I settle behind her, I start. "I'm going to wrap my arms around you, and you're going to wear my hand like your personal necklace."

She shivers, and I slide my hand under her arm to grasp around her neck. Tight as I hold her, I make sure to keep my hand curved, so the pressure is on two points on the side of her neck rather than on her airway. I have a feeling restricting her breathing might bring about a panic attack.

Her hand goes up to reach for me but only manages to reach my shoulder. Her fingers are tight there, but as I slide my other hand across her stomach, she begins to relax. I can feel the instant when everything falls into place, and she finally lets go.

Griffin watches us carefully, and the lust shining on his face encourages me to keep going.

"Tell him what you need." I speak the words quietly, so as to not overwhelm her. "Out loud, darling."

She hesitates, but when she speaks, her words are sure. "Control. I need control."

"And you, sweet boy. Can you give that to her?"

"Anything for Mistress." He is testing the title, but Juliana glows at the words.

Redirecting my attention back to the woman in my grasp, I whisper in her ear, "Juliana, take what you need. Guide him. Show him. Teach him to serve you."

XXVIII

HYPNOTIC

Griffin

Juliana exhales a quiet moan and arches her back at whatever Sage whispers. I'm wary because I don't know her well, but I have to trust she is acting in Juliana's best interest.

Calling Jules "Mistress" is definitely new, but it feels right. I want to serve her in whatever capacity she desires. I am hers to do with as she pleases.

I've never been a subservient person in the past. Twice now, I've fallen to my knees before this woman and experienced a sense of peace. My purpose is to give everything over to her, surrendering to her will, knowing she will lead me to ecstasy.

Coming to focus on me, our eyes connect. There is power there. A confidence I have yet to see from Juliana, and the shiver it sends down my spine is exhilarating.

Sage's hand is still wrapped around my mistress's throat, but it seems to comfort her rather than scare her.

Her hands are free, and my cock jumps when she reaches out to firmly fist a handful of my hair. The slight tug she gives guides me further between her thighs and closer towards her cunt.

It feels like ages since I've tasted her. Every part of me craved her when we were separated, and I longed to return to her. Between her full thighs, I feel like I have come home. But before seeking what I crave, I look up to her for permission.

"On the bed. Now." Her tone is forceful, and I scramble to fulfill her command.

When she lets go of my hair, I see her twist and mumble something in mommy's ear.

Did I call her mommy? No, Madam.

Madam places a soft kiss on Jules's forehead before releasing her from her grasp.

Realizing I stopped moving for a moment while I observed them, I rush to lie down on the bed and face them.

Both of them move to stand beside the bed next to me, but neither acknowledge me. Their gazes are locked on each other as they communicate something silently.

Slowly, Sage reaches for the buttons on Jules' dress. One by one, they come undone, but the two never take their gaze away from each other. They are in some kind of trance together.

Watching them is making my cock harden and throb with need. Unsure which I want more, I resist the urge to squirm, knowing my mistress would not approve. Though the realization that I want Sage too is new, it feels natural.

Madam's fingers slip under the dress and draw it over Jules's shoulders. When it lands on the floor, my eyes lock on the most beautiful sight.

My mistress's round breasts hang full and heavy. I want to bury my face in them and suck on her nipples hidden beneath the lace of her bra. I want to graze my teeth over them and absorb the sounds of pleasure I know she would make.

When she draws off of her underwear, Sage places her hands on Juliana's hips and leans in to speak quietly into her ear.

Suddenly, my mistress snaps her attention to me at what Sage said, and heat rages in her eyes. She looks back at the woman, searching for something, but Sage stands there as patient as ever. She is waiting for Jules to make a decision on her own. Prompting her to lead. To take charge.

Jules turns to me once more and crawls up on the bed. Swinging her leg over me, she places herself so she is perfectly straddling my hips. Her pussy perfectly aligned with my throbbing cock.

I tried to rock up into her, but with one hand, she

forces me back down.

"Please, Mistress?" I ask.

"Do you like calling me that? Do you want me to be your mistress?"

"Yes, Mistress. Please. Let me be yours." My voice is raspy with need. I can only hope she sees the truth I offer. I want to be hers. In every way that matters and in any way she needs me.

Grasping me by the chin, she looks into my eyes and soul. Searching for any sign of deception. Finding none, she releases me and reaches for my wrists, which she pulls above my head.

"No touching. Not without my permission."

I nod vigorously and wait for instructions.

She begins to rock her hips and slide her pussy up and down my aching cock. Making it hard to concentrate on her words.

"You're mine. And I will use you in whatever way I want. Got it?" She doesn't even wait for my response, knowing I would never deny her. "You're going to be a good boy and put that tongue to work, and I'm going to ride your face until I come. And if you do well, then I will ride your dick until you're begging for release." She leans in closer. "But at no point are you allowed to come without my permission."

Frozen by her words, all I can do is stare back into her gemstone eyes.

Satisfied I understand, Jules moves herself up my body and turns around to face Sage, who makes her way to the foot of the bed. The way Sage looks at us together is hungry.

Immediately, my attention is drawn back to Jules as she lowers herself down on my face.

The second she comes near enough, I lift my head and stretch to reach her pussy. I am desperate for her and have been for months.

When she's fully seated upon me, I begin to stroke her folds with my tongue. Working her lips apart with each pass I make, I find her clit and make slow circles until she rocks her hips in a pattern mirroring my own movements. A thrill rolls through me as I feel how turned on she is, but I want to make this last. So I slow my movements and reset my pace.

Clearly unhappy with the change, she grinds down further on me in frustration. I speed up in response, my tongue finding her entrance. Thrusting into her, I hear her moans of pleasure coming from above. Wanting to hear more of the sound, I mistakenly reach for her thighs to pull her closer to my face. Immediately, I feel a harsh thwack across my dick from Mistress. The sensation is both pleasure and pain. It makes my hips kick up, and I grind them into the air, hoping to find pleasure there. But there is nothing to ease the searing ache I feel.

I quickly move my hands back above me and redouble my efforts in penance. The time it takes to bring her to climax is irrelevant. I take pleasure in every groan and twist of her hips over my mouth. Each small sign of pleasure makes my pride swell, and I revel in the feeling.

I can sense when she is close to coming. Her hips rock on my mouth frantically, searching for the precipice of ecstasy, and her entire body slackens as her control dissipates. With another lick across her clit, I feel her fall, but I don't let up. Each shudder and shake of her body are evidence of her climax. I continue to lick and flick as she comes down from the high.

Finally, when she can take no more, she draws her body off me and turns to look at me dead-on.

When she speaks, my heart soars.

"Well done, pet. I think you deserve a reward," she coos as she cups my face gently.

I buck my hips up in anticipation and plead with her. "Please, let me touch you."

"No. Not yet," Jules responds, and the affection in her voice makes me swoon.

I am focusing on how Jules drags her hand down my chest, feeling my body lightly with her fingertips, when out of the corner of my eye, I see Sage reach for her. She guides Jules to straddle my hips, and I groan at the sight of her so close to my cock.

She hovers there while studying my physique and caressing every inch of skin she can reach. Leaning down to lay light kisses across my collarbone, she trails her hands up my arms and holds me by my wrists.

She guides them down so they lay perpendicular to the bed and kisses her way up my jaw before whispering in my ear. "Stay still."

I groan again in response and fist the fabric on the bed to anchor myself.

Feeling the heat of her so close to me has me unraveled, but I'm distracted. I'm not expecting it when Sage takes hold of me and begins to stroke.

I see the tenderness with which the woman touches and guides Jules. It's so careful, and I appreciate the tenderness between them.

I finally feel warmth approach my tip, and my back arches in anticipation. I am so ready for her to take me. Ready for her to use me for her pleasure.

The vision before me is breathtaking. Sage holds Jules by the hip and slowly lowers her down onto me.

"Thank you, M... Madam." I stop myself before the word slips out completely, but I know eventually I'll have to think about why the mommy thing feels so right.

"You needed that. Didn't you, sweet boy? You need your mistress desperately." The woman's words strike a chord in me that makes me gasp. It doesn't help Jules is finally seated fully on me and has begun to rock with me deep inside of her.

Each movement drives me closer to my peak, and I barely notice when Sage takes me by the ankles to reposition me with my knees bent. The position brings on a new sensation, and Jules leans closer into me still.

Unable to contain myself, my hips rise up and drive into her. I am searching for something in our connection, but I promised to obey her, and I'm not allowed to come until given permission.

My hands tighten on the sheets beneath me, my head straining to arch back and hold off for her.

A hand tightly grasps my chin and pulls me back to attention. The gaze she holds me with is fierce, and her order is clear.

Her. There is only her. My focus narrows on the woman before me. Juliana's face turns over her shoulder, and I hear some words being spoken. But I am surrounded by her and can't hear the words. My gaze caresses her whole body. Her stomach with scars and stretch marks, the color of her taut nipples and the weight of her breasts. The way her thighs grasp where we are connected. All of my senses are focused on the beautiful woman before me.

So when I feel something cool at my back entrance, I buck up forcefully in surprise. The sensation is new, and I am unprepared, but soon pressure joins the feeling, and I relax into the circling strokes at my entrance. When I feel the initial penetration, I hiss at the sudden flash of pain. As I am worked open, I start to relax and enjoy the new feeling of pleasure that comes.

My movements thrusting up into Jules slow. The feeling of being full combined with her tight hold on me sends me deep into the comfort of surrendering everything to her. A second finger is added. I let out a tiny mewl and a grin spreads across my mistress's face.

It pleases me to see it.

She shakes, and her hands move to my chest to keep herself upright. A hand comes between us, and I know she is close.

Enjoyable as it is, I pull my focus away from the stretching sensation in my ass and direct my focus back to my connection with Jules. Seeing her movements become erratic as she bucks and writhes on top of me encourages me to quicken my pace as I thrust into her. Each drive has her clenching around me, and I struggle to keep my own climax at bay. I focus on her. Only her and her pleasure to maintain my self-control. My mind is sunken deeply into my ocean of bliss when she comes. The sensations make me filled with need, and I crave more. Still, together the two women work me long after Juliana finishes.

"Fuck. Fuck me." After what feels like an eternity at the brink, I can't help but beg. "Please, I need to come."

Smiles surround me. Then everything stops.

I desperately need release, but I remember her command. I lie there, patiently waiting for Mistress and Madam's permission as their whispered voices register.

WANT

Juliana

"H**ave you ever fucked a man, darling?"**

Sage carefully holds me by my neck while I continue to ride Griffin, and she's attending eagerly to my clit. I've thought about it before —fucking a man—but the idea of having Griffin at my mercy while I drive into him is all I need to reach my peak again.

When I collapse, Griffin holds me tightly. The pressure is grounding, and I'm comforted by how he attends to me. His fingers move slowly across my skin, and his kisses in my hair are pure adoration.

When the sweat coating my body becomes too much, I roll off him to lie by his side, and he can't hide his disappointment entirely. His cock twitches frantically, and I know what he wants. All of us do.

I move to take him in hand and resume working his ass. Sage guides me for a couple thrusts of my fingers before stepping back. She trails her fingers across my shoulders before walking to the door.

"I will be right back," she mouths and then slips out the door.

With Sage gone, all of my focus is on Griffin. Every time he comes to the edge, I pause and help guide him down before continuing. The thrill that comes with witnessing his complete surrender brings back the sense of peace I've missed since Jay left.

I want more of it.

When Sage slips back into the room, she's holding a strap-on harness.

Griffin doesn't even notice when I place a kiss on his forehead before moving away. Though he definitely notices the sudden absence of my touch.

He's on the bed panting and I wouldn't have noticed another soul in the room if it wasn't for how close Sage stands by me. Then I look down at the toy in Sage's hands.

"I borrowed it. Don't think about it too hard." And then I couldn't, because her lips land on mine, and I'm lost in the sensation of her kiss. Her lips are soft, and the kiss is playful. And I miss it immediately when she steps back.

"I'll help you at every step." Her hand cups my jaw and draws my gaze to her. "You'll never be on your own, darling. Trust me on this."

And I do.

She has me step into the harness, and the way her hands brush across my legs brings back the throbbing from earlier. Every touch of hers does. When I'm finally strapped in, Sage leads me back to the bed where Griff waits oh so patiently.

He's such a good boy.

Sage leads me to the foot of the bed, puts her hands on my shoulders, and guides me as promised.

"Tell him what you need. Where you want him."

I look back at her for further instructions, but she only smiles.

"On all fours. Facing the headboard," I say. I really have no idea what I'm doing, and there is building anxiety I refuse to acknowledge.

Unaware of my inner conflict, Griffin responds immediately. He's too far away; I grasp him by the hips and pull him towards the edge of the bed. He is close enough for me to touch every inch of his artful body.

"He needs to relax," Sage says. And she's right. Griffin is buzzing with energy, and his muscles are taught. Whether it be from nerves or need.

"Have you ever been fucked before, pet?" I ask.

I don't want this to be painful for him. I run my hands up and down his back, stopping to fondle his firm ass, and slowly, he begins to sink back into the headspace I saw him go to earlier.

"No, Mistress; only by you."

Sage hands me a bottle of lube and prompts me to coat my fingers to make sure he is truly ready. As I reach to slide my fingers in, she begins to coat the silicone cock affixed to my hips. Our motions mirror each other. My fingers slide in and out of Griffin's ass while hers run up and down my cock.

"Do you want me, pet? Do you want my cock in your ass?"

I know he's ready as his moans echo around the room and his hips push back, searching for me. I take the cock from Sage's hand and line myself up with his puckered entrance.

Pushing in slowly, I watch for any sign of discomfort from the man beneath me. I see none.

Sage nudges my hips forward with the slightest pressure, and her lips appear right at the bottom of my ear.

"Do you hear this, darling? He's without words. And you alone make him this way." The elixir of her words makes me drunk with desire. "Take him, darling. Take what is yours."

I sink into Griff to the hilt. I watch his arms collapse under him, and he buries himself into the bedding as he presses back into me. The massive man beneath me is whining and moaning. He looks absorbed in the moment, and I'm honored by the amount of trust he places in me.

"Do you see him? How he responds to you?" Sage's hands move up from my hips to explore the rest of my body. "One day, when you are ready, I am going to have you ride his cock while I pound into you from behind. Like this. And you'll moan for me as he does."

I groan and stroke his spine as I thrust in and out of him. On occasion, he tries to adjust himself, and I grip his hips tightly to still him.

He is mine. Mine to control. Mine to pleasure.

When he begins to beg, I grin wickedly.

"Please, Jules. Please let me come."

I bring my hand down sharply on his ass. "That is not what you call me. Remember who you belong to."

"Mistress. I'm sorry, Mistress," he pants out. "You. I belong to you."

"Yes, you do. My pet. Mine."

The sound of skin slapping fills the room. Once I gain a rhythm, Sage's hands caressing my body move to pinch and twist my nipples, stroke my curves, and squeeze my ass. The feelings build up lust and desire, but I don't want to lose focus.

"Do you think he deserves to come?" Sage's hands pluck at my nipples as I turn to her and slow my thrust. Her eyes gleam with a wicked light, but her words are different. "It's up to you, darling."

Looking back at the man before me, I think about everything he's done. From the beginning when he didn't even know my name, until this night when he's giving me every piece of himself. I take hold of him by his hair and yank him up so his back is pressed against me.

"Do you want to come, pet?"

"Yes. Please, Mistress."

"Do you deserve it?"

At my question, he grows quiet, and I feel a flash of concern that he's misunderstood.

"I think you do." I place a kiss at the corner of his jaw. "You have been so good to me. So sweet. Careful. Protective." I pepper kisses down his neck. All the while rocking into him, slowly.

"Please."

I reach down to lightly run my fingers up his shaft and feel the precum leaking from the tip. I look over at Sage, asking her to help.

"You've been so good for your mistress, sweet boy," she responds conspiratorially.

The whimper he utters drives my own arousal higher.

"Sage is going to help you, pet. But keep your hands on the bed."

His arms straighten as he applies more pressure to where his hands lie on the bed. Sage takes him firmly in hand, and he groans loudly. It doesn't take long. His patience and self-control are impressive, but I know we are overwhelming his senses with every thrust into his ass, tug at his hair, and stroke of his cock. He won't last much longer.

His shout rings through the room as he explodes. Cum streams out of his pulsing cock onto Sage's hand and the bed. While he rides through his release, I kiss every inch of him I can reach. I want this man to know how much this means to me.

Breathless, he collapses onto the bed, and I pull out of him. Sage goes to the bathroom while I move to roll him over onto his back.

Seeing his swollen cock brings up something, and I find myself reaching for him. I carefully hold him in hand and lower my head to lick up the remaining cum on his tip. The sound he lets out is satisfying, and I lightly suck on him until his body stops shaking and he is limp with exhaustion.

When Sage returns with a washcloth, I sit up and reach for her face. Our kiss is sweet yet demanding. The salt of Griffin's release mixes with the sweetness of Sage. Her fingers come up to run through my hair, and I lean into the kiss. She holds me to her as our lips caress each other. Her mouth parts slightly, and I demand entry. Our connection grows hotter, almost frantic, until I pull away from her reluctantly.

Moving past her to the bathroom, I find myself staring directly into the large mirror. My reflection isn't one I entirely recognize. My features are the same, but something's changed. The look that's haunted me is gone. Lessened by reconnecting with Jay. Erased by this moment with Sage and Griffin.

I take off the harness and take care of the rest of my needs. When I finish, I step back into the bedroom and pause.

There on the bed lie Sage and Griffin, both on their sides. Sage is running her fingers through his hair, and the simplicity of the moment moves me. Something akin to love blooms in my chest.

I walk over to the bed and settle in behind Griffin.

I know this is a gift they've given me, and my heart clenches at the thoughtfulness.

I pull myself closer to Griffin and inhale his lemon and clove scent. My hands wander aimlessly up and down his side until he reaches for me, and we intertwine our fingers. My hand is securely in his, and my arm is draped tightly around his chest. Sage is at his front with her hand resting on my hip.

This is how we fall asleep.

DOOM

Ember

The robot before me twitches as it comes online. The project Kieran and I are working on is almost complete after endless months of slow progress. He wanted to learn more about coding and mechanics, and I'm eager to encourage his interest.

I'm proud of the kid. He's bright and curious. Wise beyond his years too.

Right now, he's off at a day camp for kids interested in coding and robotics. He should be getting home soon though. Ash left to pick him up an hour ago.

I'm going about powering down the project when my phone rings with Ash's name lighting up the screen.

"Hey, Ash. What's up. Y'all almost back? I wanna show Kieran his robot. I finally got—"

"Sage isn't picking up. Ember, he's gone," she interrupts.

I sit there for a moment, absorbing her words.

"What do you mean *he's gone*," I respond slowly.

"I mean, I went to go pick Kieran up, and the counselor said he was already picked up."

My feet are already moving me towards the door.

"Ash, *who* picked him up?" My voice is cold. I suspect the answer, but I need to hear her say it.

We talked about this extensively. It's summer, and you can't keep a nine-year-old cooped up inside all the time. So we agreed to send him to this camp. But only because we thought it would be safe.

I've never known Ash to hesitate. She's one hell of a shot, and she's always been an act first, think later kind of person. Hearing her hesitate means things are bad.

"They said his dad picked him up."

And I'm sprinting up the stairs. "Shit. Get back here. I have to tell Sage."

I check Sage's room first before remembering she'd retreated to Juliana's with Griffin.

"Sage!" I call out. I don't even bother knocking before throwing Juliana's door open wide. "Sage, Kieran's gone."

The three of them are curled up together on the bed. They are tangled together, their nakedness a reminder of their vulnerability. I feel that same tug from when we first found Juliana. A craving for connection. Not quite the same as their physical connection, but a desire for belonging. Something I haven't felt since meeting Cy.

I feel a twinge of guilt having to wake them up to this kind of news, but there's no way I can hold this back.

"Sage," I say, shaking her. "You need to wake up. Ash went to pick up Kieran and he's gone."

Clearly they had fun together because they all seem dead to the world.

"Sage! Arrick has your son! Wake the fuck up!"

This gets her attention, and she bolts upright. The fear on her face is earth-shattering.

She is already up and out of the bed going about putting on clothes. Juliana and Griffin are coming back online as I repeat, "Ash went to pick up Kieran from camp. She called and said Kieran isn't there. The camp said his dad picked him up."

"Shit," Sage says. I don't think I've ever heard Sage curse before, but it seems like a good time for her to start. "How is that possible? We filled out forms. Arrick isn't on the list we sent of who's allowed to sign him out. Shit. How did he even know Kieran was going today?"

"I told you. Arrick is obsessed. He's been hunting y'all," Griffin chimes in. "He had *me* hunting you."

"Yeah, but how would he have known where we are?" Sage's voice is so small.

That's when I finally notice Cy's joined us. "He's been having someone follow us," he says.

"What? Why didn't you tell us?" Sage exclaims.

I hear Cy mumble a small "I did tell you" under his breath.

Cy crosses his arms and plants himself in preparation for the outburst that is sure to come.

"Cy. Why the fuck didn't you say anything?" Sage's anger is building, and I can see her protective mothering instincts kick into full gear.

"No time. You were already locked in here with them two. But there was a guy who tailed us for a while when I dropped Jay off at his place." His voice is matter-of-fact, but I've known him long enough to sense the irritation underneath.

"Well, we have to go get him."

My phone chooses that moment to ring, and the whole room looks to me.

Whoever is trying to get in touch has terrible timing.

It's Jay's number that pops up on my screen, and there's a drop in my stomach.

Shitballs.

I pick up, and already I can tell by the chaotic noises in the background that this isn't going to be good.

"Juliana needs to come to the club. All y'all need to get here. ASAP," Jay barks over the noise. He sounds pained.

Then the line goes dead.

Everyone is staring at me, but my gaze goes to Juliana.

She's pulled the sheets up around her in a cocoon. Her face is pale and blank. She's terrified.

"Juliana," I coax.

She looks up at me with ghosts in her eyes and says, "This is all my fault."

DARKSIDE

Juliana

I'm on autopilot.

Everyone is moving around me, but I don't even realize I'm going through the motions. All of this—Kieran being taken by his dad, whatever is going on at the club—is my fault.

I know it.

Once we're in the cars headed towards the club, I realize I'm dressed. It takes me even longer to process why we're heading to the club in the first place.

It's only a little after five o'clock on a weekday. What can possibly be going on at Bliss that needs immediate attention? What could possibly have spooked Jay enough to call in the cavalry?

Understanding dawns as we pull up to the club.

Smoke.

Before we can even park, I'm up and out of the car, racing towards the club door.

Why is no one outside? Why hasn't the building

been evacuated?

I approach the door and reach out a hand to open it, but an arm wraps around my waist and pulls me back.

"Think this through, ti dife." Cy's voice ignites a rage in me.

How dare he stop me? How dare he question my reaction? My people, my family, are in there. Jay is in there.

"Let me go, Cy." I struggle against him, but he doesn't let up as he drags me farther away.

Sage comes up next to us and places a hand on my shoulder. I still at her touch, but only long enough for Cy to loosen his grip on me.

Cy turns away when Ember calls out to him, and I'm off the second he's distracted. I've already yanked the door open before he can respond.

The whole club is eerily silent as I call out for Jay.

Where is everyone?

I run back to my office, hoping Jay will be there, but when I arrive, the door is wide open, and no one is there.

Frantically, I begin to check other rooms.

That's when I smell it.

Natural gas.

It's mixed in with the smell of smoke, but it's there. There must be a broken pipe somewhere, and whatever fire is burning must be deep in the building if it hasn't already taken over. I can already feel the heat of it building up the temperature as I make my way further into the club.

I'm standing in the hallway when I hear voices behind me. I spin only to find a livid Cy, frazzled Ember, and Sage looking calm as ever, ready to deal with a crisis.

"Where's Griffin?" I ask.

Of course, Sage is the one to respond. "Outside on the phone with EMS. He'll be able to get people here faster. Where's Jay?"

"I don't know." I'm starting to truly panic. The smoke has tears pooling in my eyes, and I can feel myself nearing the edge of a breakdown. I don't have time to shut down. I have to find Jay. "We should check the dressing room and the rehearsal studio."

"Okay, you and Sage head to the dressing room. Ember and I will go to the studio," Cy commands. "I can smell the gas. We need to work quickly."

I'm already moving as he talks.

The door swings wide, but I stop in my tracks at the sight.

Immediately before me is Gus, our head of security, face down on the floor, and I can see blood in his short blond hair and more pooling on the carpet by his thigh.

There are a few girls passed out in front of the makeup mirrors and one on the floor by her locker. I spot Jay a few feet away and make my way to him quickly, kneeling when I reach him.

"Jay. Jay, I need you to wake up." My thoughts are racing, and my pulse is thrumming like a hummingbird. There's blood at his mouth, and a bruise is already forming on his face.

Sage is at my side a moment later, and her hand at the back of my neck helps my panic subside.

"We need to get them out of here," she says.

I nod hollowly and bend down to try hauling Jay up. As I shift him, I see it. The red soaking through his black dress shirt.

A gunshot wound.

Griffin appears in the doorway, and his eyes go wide.

"Can you get Gus?" I cry out, gesturing towards the man with my chin. Tears are coming faster.

"Shit. Yeah, I got him."

Dragging Jay out of the building is taxing, but when I get him outside and far enough away from the building, I lay him down gently. I don't want to leave him, but I also can't leave the others to handle getting everyone else out. The blood seems to have slowed. So I rip myself away, tears coming relentlessly, and force myself back into the building.

The smoke is getting worse. It seems to be coming from the kitchen, which backs up to both the dressing rooms and studio.

Explains how the gas leaked in. This was deliberate.

I run into Ember with Rosie in their arms, and Cy has one of my girls in a fireman's hold. They don't even pause as they pass me.

"There's two more in the studio. We'll be back," Ember calls out.

My whole world is upside down and it feels like everything is spinning out of control, but I don't have time to fall apart. My feet take me back to the dressing room, and I can feel the temperature rising as I get closer.

Upon swinging the door open, flames surge along the back wall. There are only two more girls left, but the flames are moving fast. I spot Stacey closest to the flames and go to grab her next. My eyes sting with all the smoke, and my lungs struggle to take in air.

Deciding it's best to get everyone out of the dressing room, I leave Stacey in the hallway and go back for the next girl. Moments later, Griffin is right behind me, and we grab both girls.

The smoke is thick, and I can't see more than a foot in front of me. I'm desperate for air, but I hold back my breath so I don't inhale any more.

Once outside, I immediately start searching for everyone. Jay is on the ground where I left him. Sage is standing over Jay, checking on him. Ember is moving one of the girls, Rosie, farther away from the building while Cy is wrapping Gus's leg wound with what appears to be the bottom of his shirt.

I run to check on Jay, but a loud pop draws my attention back to the building. I turn and see a burst of flames that forces the upper windows to shatter. I wince at the explosion and the glass scattering everywhere. All I can do is wait and watch as my second home, my sanctuary, burns.

It feels like forever before any help arrives.

Finally, I hear sirens in the distance. When the fire trucks pull into the parking lot, I let out the sob I've been holding back and lower myself to the ground by Jay.

Griffin is already moving to talk to the responders. I see him gesture towards me, and the man he's speaking with moves before me.

"You're the owner?" the fireman asks.

I nod.

"Is there anyone else left inside?"

"I don't know. I don't think so?" My voice mirrors the tremors in my hands. "Shit. We didn't check the kitchen."

The man turns away as he talks into his comms gear.

Ambulances begin to pull in then. The responders all move quickly to check on everyone. Two approach our trio, and Sage releases him to them. One remains, insistent that he see to me. I wave him off, my gaze following Jay. I'm in shock, and I can't even process his words, but when he touches me on the shoulder, I wince. Evidently, the flames dealt me some damage too.

I'm mesmerized by the sickening image of a burning Bliss.

My heart is breaking.

Sage is before me, and she looks at me with the same concern in her eyes from when we first met. She runs the back of her fingers down my cheek, and I lean into the comforting touch.

"I don't know how, but he did this," I choke out.

"Arrick." The name is soft, but it's a confirmation of what I already know.

Rage builds in me, and I focus on the feeling. For months I've barely existed, and it feels good to grasp on to the anger.

I want him to suffer.

I look around and take in everything around me.

Ambulances are everywhere. Some have already left with Gus and a few of the girls with more severe injuries. Jay is loaded into the final ambulance with an oxygen mask over his face.

"He doesn't get to do this. He doesn't get to hurt the people I love." I'm talking to myself at this point, barely aware of Sage in front of me, but I don't care.

That bastard has taken enough.

For the first time in a long time, I feel alive. Not surviving, but truly alive.

I feel like I have a purpose.

Never underestimate a woman. We only need one reason to burn the world to the ground. He's given me more than enough. My broken body was the beginning. Now he's taken Kieran, part of my new family. He burned down the one place my existing family felt safe.

He shot Jay.

If he thinks he can take anything more from me, he's made a grave mistake.

I'm done playing the victim.

He doesn't get to hurt me anymore. I won't let him.

The carnage around me grounds my fervor. But it's the final glimpse of blood on Jay's shirt as they close the ambulance doors that decides for me.

"He pays for his empire with the blood of others. I'll pay for mine in his."

ACKNOWLEDGEMENTS

I cannot express my gratitude enough to everyone who helped me along this journey. Similar to every good "why choose" novel, it would be impossible to pick just one person...

So first, I thank you, dear reader, and the BookTok community. I wouldn't be here without you. This book wouldn't exist without you. Everyone who worked on this project I met through BookTok. I made some of my closest friends through BookTok. You are my community and my home. This is truly the #BookTikTokMade.

To Amber (@nerdy.smut.bookworm), Jenna (@khaoskender), Michaela (@rubenesque.mess), and Sander (@sanderinpajamers); you were with me from the beginning, and I am so eternally grateful. You pushed me at every step, telling me I could do this, demanding new chapters, encouraging me when I was down, and letting me ramble until I answered my own questions. Without you, this book would not have made it this far. It would have stayed a story in my head for the rest of time. Thank you for everything you've done and, most importantly, your friendship.

I found in you, Rhys (@rhys.reads), the most enthusiastic reader. Thank you for reminding me why I wrote this book, for your advocacy, for your voice.

Self-publishing is a nightmare and a dream. There

are endless things to learn, and I know that I'll continue to grow each day. But shout-out to all the authors who took pity on a clueless rando from TikTok and helped me find my way: Alexis B. Osborne (@alexis.b.osborne), Becca Fogg (@beccafoggauthor), Lillian Lark (@lillianlarkauthor), Sarah Bailey (@sarahbaileyauthor), and Sarah Blue (@sarahblueauthor.) I could never have done this on my own. I asked for help, and you answered. Thank you for your wisdom.

I cannot be more appreciative of the professionals who worked on this project, Bee (@selfbybee), who helped me organize and share this book. Katie Wolf (@thekatiewolf) guided me at every step of the editing process. Sylvia Frost (@sylviafrost) and her team at The Book Brander gave me a cover to drool over. Katrina Medina (@katrina_the_narrator) is the literal voice of this book (aka. the audiobook). Thank you for all of your contributions.

Finally, to my family, who will never read this, your support means the world to me. Thank you for supporting me when I didn't have the strength to do it on my own. Thank you for teaching me the importance of doing things that bring me joy. Also, if you haven't figured it out yet, I'm bisexual. Do with that information what you will. Love ya!

And last, because it cannot be said enough to the readers and BookTok... Cheers!

ABOUT THE AUTHOR

Shannon Elliot resides in Houston, TX, with her fur baby and writes spice whenever she's not at the dog park dog or curled up with a good book. Evidenced by her background in theatre, she is drawn to story-telling and the creative process. Shannon believes that diverse and inclusive stories shouldn't be the exception, they should be the rule. Happily ever after is for everyone and she aims to write romances that reflect her readers.

Griffin's Gluten-Free Vegan Muffins

Ingridients :

2 tbsp olive oil
  (plus some to grease the tin)
2 cups almond flour
1/4 cup sugar
1 tsp baking soda
1/2 tsp Kosher salt
1/2 tsp ground cinnamon

6 tbs JUST egg
1 tsp vanilla extract
6 oz blueberry coconut yogurt
1 cup fresh blueberries

Directions :

1. Preheat oven to 425. Grease muffin tin/line with inserts.
2. In large bowl, whisk together almond flour, sugar, baking soda, salt, and cinnamon.
3. In smaller bowl, combine egg substitute, olive oil, vanilla, and yogurt.
4. Gently stir the wet ingredients into the dry ingredients. The batter will be fairly stiff. Gently fold in fruit.
5. Divide batter into the muffin tin. Bake for 5 minutes at 425.
6. Reduce heat to 350 and bake for another 15 - 20 minutes or until muffins are lightly golden and thoroughly dry on top.
7. Transfer muffin tin to a wire rack to cool before serving.